ABOUT THE AUTHOR

] Rigby, who lives in West Yorkshire, started writing
s 'y after he retired five years ago. Two local creative
١ ; groups helped him to move away from years of report
١ ' and to start writing short stories. **DARKSTONE** is
] I full length story and the first to be published.

DARKSTONE

THE FUTURE MAY BE CLOSER THAN YOU THINK

DAVE RIGBY

Matador
9 Priory Business Park
Kibworth Beauchamp
Leicestershire LE8 0RX, UK
Tel: (+44) 116 279 2299
Fax: (+44) 116 279 2277
Email: books@troubador.co.uk
Web: www.troubador.co.uk/matador

ISBN 978-1784622-107

British Library Cataloguing in Publication Data.
A catalogue record for this book is available from the British Library.

Typeset in Aldine by Troubador Publishing Ltd
Printed and bound by CPI Group (UK) Ltd, Croydon, CR0 4YY

Matador is an imprint of Troubador Publishing Ltd

DARKSTONE

December 1st

The wolf caught a scent on the breeze and walked slowly away from the icy waters of the loch, towards the darkness of the forest. In a small clearing the rough ground had been disturbed. The wolf pawed at the earth, twitched its nostrils and began digging, pushing snow, sandy soil and pine needles aside with rapid movements of its front paws. Its claws scratched against torn, black plastic and dug into exposed flesh. At the sound of approaching footsteps, the wolf stopped, turned and snarled.

Ellis froze. He couldn't see clearly. He waited a few moments until his eyes adjusted to the forest gloom. The creature was standing guard over its prey, baring its teeth, growling loudly. Ellis slowly recognised the wolf's outline. He could smell the animal; an earthy, bitter aroma. He saw the small heap of soil and realised the wolf had been digging.

He was rooted to the spot. Should he turn and run or stay and risk attack? He remained motionless. He called out and the wolf slowly turned its attention away from the ground, its growl deep and guttural. Ellis looked straight into the yellow eyes. The wolf returned his gaze, confident, unflinching, hypnotic. He stood his ground and talked to the wolf in a low voice, feeling no fear. He was puzzled. Why was it so far south? The creature began to circle slowly to the left, as if sizing up its opportunity. Ellis spoke again to the beast, telling it to walk away, to leave him be. He could sense the wolf working it out, making its decision.

The animal turned towards the spruce trees and suddenly was gone.

Ellis adjusted his cap, pulling it lower over his ears. He walked towards the rough ground, reached for a head torch from an inside pocket, strapped it to his forehead and turned it on. The strange artificial light gave the scene an unearthly glow and the pine trees beyond looked even darker. He moved closer. For a second time he froze. He tried to tell himself that the shoulder exposed under the black plastic wasn't human, but he knew it was.

He searched his pockets for his phone and in his haste, took an age to find it. He should let the authorities know. He cursed when he couldn't get a signal and wondered what he should do. He could forget about it, walk away, and refuse to get involved. He knew the risks he would be taking. He knew what *they* could be like. But if he left now, the wolf would be back. Could he really leave someone's body to that fate?

He made a decision and walked quickly through the snow, retracing his steps. The Land Rover was parked near the loch. He opened the passenger door and grabbed a shovel, telling himself the whole time that he was doing the right thing. When he reached the clearing again, he started digging carefully around the body. It was hard, hot work, the sweat dripping inside his clothes, turning cold immediately, chilling him. The body was almost fully covered in black plastic. He unsheathed the knife on his belt and slit the covering. He stood back and stared at the corpse. It was a woman, tall, thin, not long in her resting place.

He suddenly thought about how it might look. Would they try and pin a murder on him? He took a photo of the gruesome scene with his phone: the body, the shallow grave and the surrounding trees. He gritted his teeth and stooped low to lift the corpse onto his shoulder. It was heavier and more awkward than he'd anticipated. But the vehicle wasn't far away and he was able to reach it without stopping. He kept a wary eye open for the wolf but there was neither sign nor scent of the creature. He opened the back of the Land Rover and slid the body in. There was just enough room alongside the chainsaw and the axe. The deep brown eyes set in a worn face seemed to be staring right through him.

As he tied the loops on the Land Rover's canvas cover and secured the final one over the steel peg, he thought again of the wolf. He realised he was shivering.

The vehicle started first time. That made a nice change. He drove slowly over the tree roots, up the slope, keeping in four-wheel drive. The headlights jerked up and down. The forest looked like a stage set, two-dimensional. The snow started falling again and the windscreen wipers struggled to keep up. Where was he going? He knew it would be no good going to the Brigade locally. They wouldn't have a clue and would probably arrest him for murder. He'd have to make the long drive to Glasgow. He thought about his father and the Brig. He hadn't really had any contact with them since that awful time.

It took him almost two hours to reach the street lights. The snow had stopped. The road surface was slippery but manageable. He tried to recall the route to the Brig's West End station – down the Great Western Road and right onto Byres Road seemed best He glanced nervously at the fuel gauge. This was an unplanned journey which would eat into his monthly ration. Eventually, he saw the neon sign up ahead and pulled off onto the forecourt. There were automatic doors at the entrance – a surprising luxury. A rush of warm air greeted him and he unzipped his waterproof and fleece. There was a queue at the counter, the usual mix of drunk and drugged men and a couple of scantily dressed women. Ellis ignored their looks and the comments as he pushed his way straight to the front of the queue. The sergeant in military fatigues was about to tell him where to go, when he heard Ellis' simple statement.

"I've got a body in the back of my car."

The sergeant ordered two privates to flank Ellis as they walked to his vehicle in the floodlit car park. The three uniforms stared open-mouthed at the body, the chainsaw and the axe for a few blank moments, before the sergeant ordered his men to carry the body to the mortuary. He led Ellis into an interview room and after making a brief phone call, stood rigidly and silently by the door. Ellis looked round the room. There were stains on the lino. He couldn't quite determine their origins but they didn't auger well. The walls were bare apart from a photograph of the King. The venetian blinds were filthy and broken. A small man in a dark suit entered the room. The sergeant looked immediately apprehensive, but the newcomer ignored him, pulled a seat up to the red, formica-topped table and lit a cigarette. He coughed, spat and rubbed the spittle into the floor with the toe of his shoe. There were no introductions.

"You've got five minutes to convince me you're not a killer," the small man said.

Ellis knew better than to talk of solicitors. He knew from bitter experience what the Brigade was capable of. He described exactly what had happened. He showed the man the pictures he'd taken on his phone. When he mentioned the wolf, his interrogator interrupted.

"There aren't any wolves that far south." Wolves had been deliberately encouraged further north – as part of the plan to drive people away from the Outland areas.

"That's what I thought," Ellis said calmly. "But, you'll just have to take my word for it. What reason have I got for making it up?"

The sergeant whispered something to the interrogator.

"Why do you have a chainsaw and an axe in the back of your vehicle?"

"Because I'm a forester." Ellis held his breath. Would the man believe him or would he be locked up? The man looked him up and down.

"OK you can go. Leave your details with the sergeant."

"Look, about the woman, can you tell me who she is, when she's identified? If she's got a family, I'd like to visit them, tell them about her, help to put their minds at rest if I can." Ellis addressed this to the back of the small man as he was leaving the room. Without turning the man spoke.

"That's none of your business," he said coldly as he disappeared.

Ellis drove home, his eyes glued to the fuel gauge. Snow was falling heavily again, the traffic was light. As he neared home, his headlights picked out the security fencing, mile after mile. He reached the empty village, turned off the road and drove slowly and carefully up the track over fresh snow to his house.

Laska emerged from the wood shed to greet him, tail wagging furiously. Ellis unloaded the tools and locked them in a steel storage unit. He unlocked the front door and was relieved to see that the stove was still alight. He fed more logs into it and damped it down for the night. He couldn't summon up the energy to cook.

He unlaced his boots, removed them and put his feet up on the long sofa. This was covered in blankets to hide various holes and stains and he wrapped them round his cold body and fell asleep. He was awoken by the dog licking his nose, his way of asking for food. Reluctantly Ellis staggered to his feet and found the remains of a rabbit in the fridge. He mixed this with some biscuit and placed the food in a worn enamel bowl. The food disappeared rapidly. Ellis was asleep again in seconds.

December 2nd

It was hard to tell if it was morning. It was one of those winter days which never really gets going, where you wait for a little more light but it never comes. Ellis lay on the sofa, staring at the ceiling, his mind blank. It slowly dawned on him that yesterday had not been an ordinary day. He thought of his father and the Brig. He thought of his own decision years ago, to cut himself off, and not get involved. But what else could he have done when he'd found the body? He could see the wolf as if it was right in front of him, there in the kitchen, staring, hungry. Was it the only one, or had others reached his forest?

His phone rang. It was a customer wanting fence poles. He could collect, which meant that Ellis could save fuel. He washed quickly and sparingly in cold water, changed his shirt and underpants and finished dressing. He went out into the yard and used the dipstick to check the level in the diesel tank. It was depressingly low and he didn't know when the next delivery would be. At least he had food. He cooked eggs and bacon and ate straight from the frying pan, mopping up the remains of egg yolk and grease with a thick slice of bread. He and the dog sat warming themselves, contentedly, by the stove.

He wondered about making the call. He knew he should leave well alone. As the Brig detective had said, it was really none of his business. But there was a nagging voice in his head. He wanted to know more. The Brigade would probably go through the motions of investigating but he could imagine them dropping the case if no-one was likely to kick up a stink. Just another violent death – no doubt linked to drugs or illegal immigration. His father's voice told him to dial the number.

"Mrs Lambert? Hi, it's Ellis, do you remember, Ross' old friend. Yes it's a long time. No I'm afraid she died just over three years ago. Very difficult. Listen, I'd like to contact Ross if I could. I need some advice. Would you be able to give me his number, his personal mobile if possible?" He copied down the number onto a scrap of paper. "That's really helpful. Thanks, Mrs Lambert – yes that would be nice. Bye."

He hadn't spoken to Ross Lambert for several years. They'd been close as students, but had drifted apart. He didn't know what sort of job Ross did in the Brig but maybe he would be able to get hold of the information he needed.

"Ross! It's Ellis, yes, that Ellis. No, I know – too long." He told Ross what had happened, what he wanted and gave him the number on the receipt he'd been given by the Brigade. Even a corpse had a receipt. He was cautious, explaining it was just the concern of one human for another, nothing more. Ross sounded equally cautious, probably didn't want to get involved.

"It'll depend on whether they've got prints or not. If they have, then an address should be no problem. Without prints you could be waiting a long time. Mind you, the number of prints we've got these days…" Ross trailed off. "Why don't we meet up anyway – the old breakfast place, catch up a bit?"

Ellis tried to pick up the underlying tone in his friend's voice. Was this a rebuff or was there something else?

"Two hours' time suit you?"

Ellis asked him to make it three.

He knew he wouldn't have sufficient fuel for the whole journey. He fitted the wire screens to the windscreen and the side windows of the Land Rover, just in case and drove as far as the railway station at Alexandria. There were only two other vehicles in the car park.

The train was delayed. An old man sat on a bench, head bowed, trussed up in a navy blue overcoat, his bare hands red-raw. When the train finally arrived, he rose stiffly and wearily to his feet and shuffled to the nearest door. Ellis helped him mount the step and the man nodded his thanks. There were few other passengers in the carriage. People couldn't afford the fares. The train rattled slowly towards the city, stopping frequently, as if waiting for imaginary expresses that never arrived. The man smelled of stale tobacco and humbugs. Ellis asked him where he was going, just to make conversation. The man didn't reply but stared mournfully out of the window occasionally wiping his nose with a large dirty handkerchief. Ellis gave up trying to be sociable and resorted to window gazing. They passed tower blocks, some abandoned, others fenced off, painted bright colours, teeming with life. When they reached Queen Street Station, Ellis glanced across to where the old man had been sitting. His seat was empty. Perhaps he'd got off at one of the earlier stations.

Ellis walked briskly to Central Station. The concourse was full of people, bags, cases, stalls, noise and the sounds of music. A piper was plying his trade in the far corner. His kilt had seen better days. He had a small wiry dog at his side, curled up on a tartan rug. The dog appeared to be dreaming and his body shook periodically. The piper got lost mid-tune and stuttered to a halt, replacing his mouthpiece with a roll-up.

Ellis made his way across the big open space towards Brucciani's. He decided he was going to indulge himself and have a coffee. This was a luxury. He couldn't remember the last time he'd treated himself. He sat at a small table by the door and sipped the dark brew slowly, enjoying every minute of it. A tall man with short dark hair and a neatly trimmed beard held out his hand to Ellis. He hadn't changed at all in the intervening years.

"Great to see you Elly. How are you coping with the big city?" Ellis grasped the hand and shook it warmly.

"Can't remember the last time I came into town twice in two days. Sorry to have put you on the spot about the woman's details. I know it's difficult for you."

"No bother, big man. I just didn't want to do it over the phone. There's random recording so you never know when. Anyway, you're in luck. Her prints were on file, so we know who she is already. Her name's Carla Lucini, registered at her parents' house out in Paisley. Here's the address. Don't have any other information though."

Ross passed a small piece of paper across the table. Ellis glanced at it, before putting it into his jacket pocket.

"That's really good of you, must put you out on a limb a bit."

"Don't worry, I've covered my tracks. Don't forget I used to be a techie, still keep my hand in. Something to eat?"

The small café had been their regular meeting point in their student days, post-clubbing. They felt at ease there. Ellis decided to splash out on the bruschetta.

The Paisley train was even older than the one he'd caught earlier. As it left the station, the train from London slid in to his left, all gleaming metal and windswept looks. They crossed the Clyde and Ellis watched the barge traffic through the grimy windows. He glanced across to the other side of the carriage and was surprised to see the old man from the first train, but this version of him was talking animatedly to a young woman. He nodded in the man's direction but he showed no signs of recognition. He checked the location of Ainslie Park in his A to Z, didn't want to be seen on the estate pulling out a street map. It wasn't far from the station. He could walk there. The train reached Paisley and Ellis pulled his coat collar up and wound his scarf a little more tightly around his neck.

Ainslie Park was a Class Two estate, so it might be difficult, but it would be covered by a local Vigi Patrol which gave him some comfort. At least it wasn't a Class Three run by the local gangs. He knew there'd be no sign of the Brigade who'd left the old council estates to their own devices.

He saw a Patrol as it marched past, dark uniforms, berets, large boots. They were generally OK, but weren't averse to running protection rackets and smuggling fags and booze. Better though, than the anarchy that had come before. He turned into Fraser Drive and hesitated whilst he worked out the numbers. 72A was an upstairs flat. The front door was on the side of the building. Ellis rang the bell and it sounded in the distance. He heard heavy footsteps coming slowly down the uncarpeted stairs. The door was opened by a woman who looked to be in her mid-seventies, short, straggly grey hair, holding an over-fed cat to her bosom. The woman peered at him and then told him she didn't want whatever it was he was selling.

"Sorry to disturb you," he started off hesitantly. He realised he hadn't really planned what to say. "I'd like to talk to you about your daughter, Carla."

The woman hesitated for a moment, as if weighing up whether she could trust this stranger on her doorstep. The she beckoned him into the tiny hallway. There was an awkward little dance ending with her leading the way up the stairs. The cat stared at him malevolently over the woman's shoulder. Ellis reached the top of the stairs and found himself in a living room of sorts. There was a central aisle flanked on either side by piles of old, yellowing newspapers, discarded clothes and empty cans and bottles. The walls were bare – no pictures or photographs. A wizened man sat in a worn armchair staring at a blank TV screen.

"He's waiting for Countdown," the woman said wearily. "Can I get you a cup of tea?"

Ellis had to concentrate to follow what she was saying, her accent a strange mix of Scots and Italian. He accepted her offer of a drink. Had their daughter really lived here? There was no trace of a younger person in the room. The tea arrived in a large chipped mug which advertised the Barras market. Sugar was still cheap and there was plenty in the milky brew. He sipped it slowly.

"Have you had a visit from the Brigade at all?" Ellis waited. The woman looked towards the seated man, but he continued to stare at the screen.

"No, we've not heard from them. She's never been in trouble with them." The woman again looked at her husband. "Of course we don't see much of her, although she was here the other day."

Ellis thought this was odd, as the flat was her registered address.

The old woman paused. "It's bad news isn't it?"

Ellis swallowed. There was no easy way of doing this. Clearly the Brig hadn't bothered to break the news to the next of kin, just as he'd suspected. He explained what had happened, giving the woman a highly edited account of the events of the previous day. She stared at him as if he was making it all up. He had to admit that even he found it difficult to believe the story.

"How do they know it was her?" was all she said. He told her about the fingerprints and made up a story about the Brig asking him to visit and break the news. A single tear trickled slowly down her cheek. Her husband turned round slowly to face her.

"I always feared she'd come to a nasty end," he said and turned back to the blank screen. The woman wiped her face and grasped Ellis' hand.

"Don't listen to him. Half the time he's not with us anyway. She's never been in any trouble. I can't understand why they already had her fingerprints. She had so much to live for. And what'll I do now?"

"I could try and find out a bit more if you like," said Ellis, trying to silence the voice in his head telling him to leave well alone. The woman nodded her assent and her gratitude.

"Where did she work?"

"Oh, she worked with all that website stuff, media, you know. But I can't recall the name of the company. She was away a lot. I never did really understand what she did."

"When did you last see her?"

"Well, let me think, maybe it was yesterday. No, it was the day before, because I remember now, she helped me put the bin out."

"Did she mention anything particular when she was here?" The woman paused, trying hard to remember.

"Not really. Oh, wait a minute, she said something about a man she'd just met. I was pleased, because she doesn't seem to meet many men. Now, what was his name?" Her face fell and she struggled to keep herself together. Her husband sat there without saying a word.

"Ah that was it – Gordon, nice name. She said he had long ginger hair which seemed a pity. I don't like the long hair. I think he's something to do with websites as well. Lives in the West End she told me. Has a bit of money I dare say."

"Did she give you any idea whereabouts in the West End?"

"I think she said he lived in one of the blocks near Partick station. Of course we never met him. I just can't believe it – my poor little Carla."

They talked quietly for a while longer. At 3:30 exactly the man pressed a button on the remote and the TV blared into life with a theme tune Ellis vaguely recognised. He said his farewells and made his way down the stairs and out of the front door.

As he retraced his steps to the station, he kept a wary eye on the opposite pavement. Two figures in hoods and baseball caps, trousers tucked into socks, phones held like weapons, were loping along, glancing in his direction. He slowed slightly and then crossed the road to slot in behind them. They'd lost the initiative and were unsure how to respond. As they reached the junction with the main road, they drifted off, leaving Ellis to wander back to the station to catch his train.

He was surprised Carla's mother had been so open with him. Perhaps she just welcomed the chance to talk to someone. But he didn't have much hard information to go on, just a few details about the boyfriend and a rough location. It would probably be a waste of time but he'd give it a go anyway.

+ + +

"We'll have to take the site down, take a breather and start again. But we can concentrate on the zine in the meantime."

Gam kept his gaze fixed on the screen in front of him as he made a series of rapid key strokes. He was tall and looked under-fed. But his eyes were intense and he gave off a nervous energy. He wore a pinstripe suit that had seen better days, a pink shirt open at the neck and trainers over his bare feet.

"We haven't got any choice really. Was it the usual?" Colette lay stretched out on the sofa, shielding her eyes from the fluorescent light above. She was in her early thirties, a runner's frame, her short hair streaked with purple.

"Pretty much – D17 again. Do you fancy a drink before we head up north?"

Colette agreed and they collected their jackets and headed for the door. They were much practised in the walk down from the sixth floor and couldn't remember the last time the lift had worked. Most of the other repairs, the Dalkeith Gardens Block Committee could sort out themselves but they couldn't get the parts for the lift.

They emerged on to the street, picking their way round the slush and the potholes. The street lights had long since been turned off in their neighbourhood, but there was sufficient light from the shops and workshops for them to see their way. Later in the evening it would be a different story.

The Old Delight was a traditional boozer, an old man's pub as Colette called it. The beer was good and it was cheap, unlike the up-market bars that the suits frequented. It was at the end of a cul-de-sac.

As they reached the dimly-lit front door, two men stepped out of the shadows and intercepted them. The burly one spoke.

"Now then – off for a nice quiet drink are we? Well we'd like a wee conversation with you Mr Mossman, so the Deuchars will just have to wait."

Gam was led down an alleyway, then across an area of rough ground to a car with darkened windows. As he was shoved inside, his head caught the edge of the front passenger door. Almost instantly, he could feel the swelling above his eye. He wondered what had happened to Colette.

A thickset man in Brig fatigues, half turned to face him from the driver's seat. He wore dark glasses even though they were surrounded by gloom. He smoked continuously and tapped a pen against a clipboard which held a single piece of paper.

"You never learn, Mossman, do you? Still trying to stir things up with your pathetic website. Why don't you drop this nonsense? My boys are round at your place confiscating your laptop right now. What I want to know is where your gen comes from, who are your informants?"

Gam stared past the dark glasses. He was used to this. It was like a game, not a pleasant one, but he knew how it ended. He would give the Brig a little information, useless, out of date stuff and they would make things uncomfortable for him, usually in the area of his midriff where it wouldn't show. They'd slipped up this time. The swelling above his eye was a little prominent. Not that it would bother them unduly.

He leant back in his seat. He fed them some snippets of information, details of a demo on World Democracy Day, which they'd already decided to cancel and the web address of an anarchist site, which had just been deactivated. He contemplated releasing some more information about Nash, who was still in custody, but decided to save it for a future occasion. He breathed out hoping he'd said enough.

The silk scarf was slipped around his neck so quickly, that he didn't have time to move. He gasped for breath as it tightened round his throat. They were getting serious, they weren't playing any longer. He coughed, which only made things worse. At last the pressure eased and he fell forward, doubling up in his seat.

"Just a little warning, you understand," the driver said. "I know the garbage you've given me is just that. I expect more. You've got a couple of days. We know where to find you".

The driver gave the slightest of gestures. The passenger door opened and Gam was manhandled from the car and led back down the passageway. He heard the sound of a high-powered engine being revved before it faded into the distance. Who was that man? Gam was certain he'd not seen him before.

A sudden weakness hit him. He managed to walk the few yards to the Old Delight and order a dram. He collapsed into a chair. He felt the cool hand of Colette on his forehead. She hadn't been harmed. She'd had the nice cop treatment – *just a bit of co-operation, that's all we're after. Just have a word with your man, make him see reason.*

She asked the barman for some cotton wool and disinfectant. He rummaged around in the back room and emerged with a small green bottle and two fluffy balls. Colette bathed around the swelling and told Gam he'd live.

"Good job there's nothing much on the laptop," he said, adding that it would now be in the hands of the Brig. He rubbed his neck and downed the shot.

The pub was a real refuge, no screen, no music, just a slowly ticking clock on the mantelpiece above the log fire. Gam had no idea where the landlady found the fuel. Open fires were a rarity in the city. They drank pints in long straight glasses.

"We'd best be setting off," Gam said as they finished their drinks.

A few older men were standing at the bar. They knew Gam and something of his reputation. They weren't exactly supporters but they certainly weren't informers.

"Any diesel available?" Gam asked the group. One of the men nodded and reached for his wallet. He pulled out half a dozen coupons and Gam paid him the usual rate. There was no need for haggling.

When they returned to the flat, it was in the expected state, belongings strewn about for fun, mattress ripped apart, toilet blocked. They couldn't face clearing up, but packed a few things and walked the short distance to the lock-up. The old Transit started first time. Gam reached around the back of the Tracka box and plugged in the simulator. He didn't want the Brig to know their true destination. Of course they ran the risk of immediate imprisonment if they were caught.

Colette eased the van out onto the rutted forecourt. They glanced at the map in the torchlight and agreed on the route. At the Bearsden service station, they joined the queue and waited. They'd gambled that by driving out of the city centre there'd be more of a chance of fuel. Eventually they reached one of the pumps and used their maximum quota. The cashier stared at the coupons and held them up under the ultraviolet light. Forgeries were commonplace. He nodded and they drove out onto the darkened road, north. They'd stop for something to eat at a fish farm they knew on the way.

"So what do you know about this Meikle feller?" Colette asked.

"Well he sounds OK, says all the right things. That's why I want to meet him and his group. They're in the middle of nowhere so the Brig don't bother them. It's not worth their while."

Gam glanced in his mirror again, but couldn't see any following headlights. He'd been worried about a green BMW a few miles back but it seemed to have turned off. Traffic was thin. Colette drove steadily. There was no rush.

They stopped at the fish farm and ordered smoked salmon sandwiches. The shop and café were both closed, but Gam knew the owners and they were happy to see him and Colette and feed them for their onward journey.

"How's business?" Gam asked, trying to get his mouth round the fish-filled baguette.

"It's like all food nowadays," his friend said. "We can't produce it quick enough. We don't get too much of a problem with poaching up here. We're well fenced and few people live round these parts now. There are some roughnecks up in the hills but we came to an agreement. We let them have the stuff they need cheaper than usual and they leave us alone. Where are you headed?"

Gam was uncertain how to answer. It wasn't that he didn't trust the fish farmer. But if the Brig started snooping around, the fewer people that knew about their movements – the better.

"Well you know what it's like these days. We're not exactly flavour of the month with the Brig. So it's probably better if you don't know about our destination."

His friend nodded and almost smiled, "I'm not exactly on their party invitation list either."

They stocked up with some dried and tinned food and set off north. An hour later, they went over a small narrow bridge and Colette flashed the headlights three times and then waited. She repeated the flashes and then saw the answering lights off to their right, half way up the hillside. She followed the track which was in poor condition. They just about made it over the gap-toothed cattle grid and laboured up the steep hill, eventually pulling in to a compound and drawing up between two old ambulance vehicles.

A squat man with bare arms covered in tattoos strode across the worn concrete towards them. He seemed hostile, but Gam assumed this was probably just his usual look

"I'm Meikle. You must be Mossman. Expected you earlier. Come on in."

Gam exchanged knowing glances with Colette and they followed their host across the compound to a ramshackle farmhouse. Smoke was pouring from a leaning chimney. Two oil lamps hung from metal hooks either side of the low doorway. The living room was a mess, plates, dishes, mugs and glasses scattered across the floor and any available surface. Meikle tipped a sleeping cat off one of the armchairs, moved a box of tools off a second and beckoned for his visitors to be seated.

"So, did you bring the Brig with you?" The accent was Aberdonian. The man flexed his muscles every now and then and looked permanently tense.

"I shook them off about thirty miles back." Gam didn't see any point in elaborating. "We'd like to do a bit of a feature on you and your group," he continued. "I hear you've been actively recruiting."

"We've hardly started," Meikle said with almost a sneer. "Once we get properly set up, you'll be impressed. They'll all be impressed. Of course we'll need cash for more hardware, so I plan to hit one of the banks." This wasn't at all what Gam had expected to hear.

"How do you plan to do it?" Colette asked hesitantly.

"Sorry, can't go into operational detail," Meikle said, tapping the side of his nose. "Anyway you'll be OK sleeping here." It was a statement, not a question. He tossed them a couple of threadbare blankets. "We're up at seven by the way."

With that he left the room and they heard him shouting loudly to someone as he mounted the stairs. Luckily they'd bought sleeping bags, which they rolled out onto the floor. They tried to ignore the sounds of energetic sex from the room above.

December 3rd

Even by eight the next morning, the house was still completely quiet. Colette managed to find some milk which wasn't off and they used their own tea bags to make a brew. They found enough room in the kitchen sink, which was full of dirty dishes, to rinse a couple of mugs. The room looked worse in the daylight.

They talked in low voices about how the trip had turned out to be a waste of time. On his website Meikle talked a good game, coherent, articulate, well-reasoned. But it was a different picture on the ground. Gam worried about the damage Meikle's group would cause.

"Meikle's a bloody godsend for the Brig. He'll provide the perfect excuse for yet another clampdown. Why do they insist on scoring so many own goals?"

Colette knew he didn't really expect an answer. She just touched his arm gently.

They sat outside the farmhouse on a rickety bench, trying to warm themselves a little in the thin sun. A figure appeared suddenly beside them. Neither of them had heard him arrive.

"So, is comrade Meikle showing you his usual hospitality?"

"Well he wasn't here to greet us at seven as promised, that's for sure. I'm Mossman, this is Colette".

"I'm Kilbride – number two here. We're a bit rough and ready but we get things done."

"What's your speciality?" Gam looked towards the other man

as he asked the question. He had a feeling he'd seen him before somewhere. He seemed to have no neck.

"Oh, we keep the information pretty tight up here. Let's just say I'm an organiser. Now, how about some breakfast?"

Kilbride went to one of the outbuildings and returned with milk, bread, eggs, butter. He swept the dirty plates off the range and a few minutes later, tea, toast and omelettes were in front of them. He talked all the while, emphasising the importance of their 'operations' as he called them, without ever being specific. When they sat down at a cleared corner of the table, he suddenly switched to asking the visitors about their 'operation'. Gam was deliberately vague. He instinctively didn't trust this man, didn't want to give anything away. Several times Kilbride asked for particulars, but Gam batted away these enquiries, using a jokey approach, as if their feeble activities didn't amount to much. Colette kept silent. She too was suspicious of Kilbride who seemed altogether out of place in the clutter and chaos of the farmhouse.

By the time Meikle emerged, unshaven, bleary eyed, wearing only jogging pants despite the cold, they'd finished the meal, washed up and cleared away and were about to set off on a "wee tour" as Kilbride had put it. Meikle barely acknowledged them. He stumbled around barefoot trying to locate anything edible or drinkable before waving a hand in their direction and disappearing back upstairs.

Kilbride made no comment. He led them to the outbuildings, unlocked one of them and took them inside. A wooden rack had been constructed along one wall of the old barn which held a range of small arms. Kilbride was clearly very proud of them and told his guests how they would soon be put to good use. Gam asked him what he meant, but he didn't elaborate, just smirked and patted the weapons. Outside again, they looked down the valley. The view was impressive. They could see the loch in the distance and the railway snaking northwards. There were few other signs of habitation. Most of the land was covered in forest.

"Well, thanks for the briefing," Gam said, trying to look and sound serious. "I'm sure we can use your information to good effect. But it's time we were moving on. Could you say our farewells to Meikle?"

Kilbride looked surprised that they were leaving so soon. "Of course – no problem. No need to remind you not to mention the hardware."

He waved them off down the rutted track and watched the van as it bump-started at the third attempt.

+ + +

Ellis couldn't get his encounter with the wolf out of his mind. It seemed so unreal. The wind was strong and he leaned into it as he traversed the ridge overlooking Loch Airne. There was snow underfoot and he kept his eyes open for tracks. He picked out squirrels, small birds and a fox, but no larger creatures. The moon shone across the water.

He pushed his hands deeper into his pockets and bent his head. Passing the clearing where he'd made his grim discovery, he thought about Carla. He wanted to know more about her. He'd made one or two initial enquiries about her friend "Gordon" in the bars and shops around Partick station, but he had so little to go on.

He pushed on towards the loch side and stood on the shore, slowly skimming pebbles across the thin ice. They made an almost metallic sound as they slid across the frozen surface. He reached inside his coat for the hip flask and swallowed a few drops of the warming liquid. He could smell the spruce, fresh and earthy. He heard the screech of an owl in the distance and then saw it as it swooped across the inlet.

He stood still, despite the cold, and thought about his father and his resistance to the steadily creeping repression, his refusal to stay quiet. Of course he'd eventually been taken in. When the Brig had released his father after that first round of interrogation, Ellis had barely recognised him, swollen eyes and lips, blood covering his face and clothes, limping badly and coughing. But he'd refused to give the Brigade the information they'd wanted. When he'd been locked up after that joke of a trial, Ellis had known he wouldn't make it. His health had never been good anyway. His heart had always had a weakness.

After his father's death, Ellis had made a decision to close his eyes to what was happening in the country, not to get involved anymore. He cut himself off and sought refuge and solitude at Kintrawe House, the old family home which had been standing empty and neglected. He repaired the house, picked up his forestry skills, bought sheep and chickens, and the dog. He'd lost Tora as a result. She couldn't cope with the isolation. He still saw her now and then but it wasn't the same.

As he turned to retrace his steps, he saw the wolf standing there, eyeing him. Ellis could see the creature's breath in the moonlight, could smell him. He spoke slowly to the wolf, about how it was good to meet up again, about what a fine night it was. The wolf sat on its haunches and cocked its head on one side as if it was taking all this in. Ellis squatted down. He reached in his pocket for the raw meat. He knew he shouldn't be doing this, encouraging the creature to visit again, but he couldn't stop himself. He threw the meat forward. The wolf backed away at first, but then moved forward, sniffing carefully, before suddenly snatching the meat, chewing and swallowing, keeping its eyes on Ellis.

Later, Ellis couldn't really remember how long they'd faced each other. He gave the wolf a name – Lucas. It was more personal rather than thinking of him as just 'the wolf'. He'd only closed his eyes momentarily, but Lucas had chosen that moment to disappear.

Ellis suddenly realised he was cold – all that sitting around. He banged his arms across his chest to get warm and broke into a slow loping run, slipping occasionally on the snow. He practised howling at the moon and felt his rendition was acceptable. As he approached the lights of his house he realised he'd reached a decision. He would stop cutting himself off.

He eased off his boots in the sudden warmth of the kitchen and placed them to dry by the stove. He needed food. There was some vegetable curry left in the fridge. Its spicy heat reinvigorated him. He pulled out a pad from the desk drawer and, using pen and ink, he sketched his new friend sitting in the snow, using a little poetic licence to add to the background a crescent rather than a full moon. He was pleased with his efforts and pinned the picture up on the corkboard by the backdoor. He wondered what he should do next. He felt his earlier resolve beginning to waver. He had so little to go on. Should he just drop his enquiries? After all it wasn't as if he'd ever known this Carla woman.

He felt his father's presence, there at the table, speaking in a low voice.

"Of course it's up to you son. But I'm not sure you'll settle until you know what happened to the young woman. She's got under your skin hasn't she?" He was looking around the kitchen, taking everything in. *"You'll be OK. You've got a good setup here."*

The vision faded and Ellis was left staring at an empty chair. This wasn't the first time it had happened – far from it. It had started shortly after his father's death. It was usually when he had a big decision to make – that soft reassuring voice. His father was right. She had got under his skin.

He made his third journey into the city the following morning. There wasn't a lot of work on at this time of year and he knew he'd be able to catch up the following week. He drove through the Outlands to Alexandria station. Most of the area was classed as unmaintained – all the services were concentrated in urban areas. The roads were potholed, schools closed, very few services available. It was the way the authorities had coped with continual cutbacks – by concentrating services in the urban areas.

The train was slow and late arriving into Glasgow, but he was in no hurry. Laska walked by his side as he made his way in and out of the shops and cafes near Partick Station, his starting point. He was trying to avoid having to knock on doors in the run-down blocks behind the station.

The snow had melted away on the city streets. The sky was a clear blue, the air still. Brightly coloured flowers in black plastic buckets were lined up outside one of the smaller shops, blooms flown in from another world. Ellis took one of the free papers from the stand outside the off-licence. The front page headline was about a body found in the River Kelvin. The man was described as a drunk, meaning the Brigade wouldn't have to bother too much trying to find out what had happened to him.

Ellis gave the dog a biscuit and they moved on to a hardware store. These had flourished over recent years. People tended to do their own repairs these days, as they couldn't afford to pay proper tradesmen. Many of the tools for sale were second hand, but there was a good market for them. The DIY approach extended in other directions, from getting a haircut to basic dentistry, for those who were really desperate.

Ellis looked through a blue plastic basket holding a range of wood chisels. He didn't need another one, but just liked the shape and feel of them. He asked the man in the brown coat behind the counter whether he knew a local man called Gordon, long ginger hair, worked in the media. He received the usual blank stare.

As he was leaving the shop a woman, who looked to be in her

mid-thirties, stopped him and said she'd overheard his enquiry. She knew someone who fitted his description. She thought he produced some kind of online magazine. He lived in the same block of flats as she did. She gave Ellis the address.

She didn't walk away but continued to stand near to Ellis and rummaged through a cardboard box full of hairdryers. He wasn't quite sure why, but the next thing he knew he was asking her if she'd like a cup of tea. He couldn't afford two coffees, but tea was manageable.

They sat at a small table at the back of a run-down café in one of the alleyways. It was cheery enough with bright red curtains and an unshaded fluorescent light. They talked about the weather, the body in the river and Ellis' dog. She said she was glad he'd asked her for a drink – she'd been on her own since her partner had left and just wanted the opportunity to talk to someone. She hoped he didn't think she was being forward. Ellis thought it was a nice old-fashioned expression. He said he had an equal need for conversation. He couldn't put his finger on what it was about her that he found attractive, her voice, her manner, but he felt instantly at ease. He patted Laska's head as they spoke and fed him a piece of the homemade shortbread that he'd ordered with the teas.

She told him a little bit about Gordon. Ellis said he'd try the flat and see if he could catch him. They walked together to Dalkeith Gardens. Any greenery implied by the name had long since disappeared and the two adjacent blocks had been demolished, leaving ugly rubble-strewn scars. Gordon's flat was empty. Ellis scribbled a note giving a brief message and his contact details. He tried to push it through the letterbox, but it was sealed up. Not surprising really, what with the mania for security and the infrequent postal service. Most people had to collect their mail anyway. He slipped the note under the door instead. He said goodbye to the woman as she put the key into the lock of her own front door two floors below.

"By the way, I'm Lorna," she said as she pushed the door open. "Let me know if I can help at all."

Ellis and the dog returned to the station and sat together in silence on the journey home.

December 4th

John Knox House, the Brigade headquarters, was a large office block close to Central Station. Standing at the fourth floor window and craning his neck, Charles Daid could just see the Clyde, the big commercial barges moving silently up and downstream, their flags fluttering in the breeze.

He flicked through the papers on his desk. They all told the same story of increasing competition. How things had changed since the easy, early days of the Brigade. They'd taken over from the police, who, after one failure too many, had been reduced to providing little more than a traffic cop service. But the original army roots of the Brigade were withering away fast as privatisation took hold.

Daid felt reasonably confident about holding onto the Strathclyde contract. It was a large and difficult patch and it was easy to get the costing badly wrong. *Great Wall* had recently won the Forth contract and Aberdeen had fallen to *Zonal Reach* a year ago. There was talk of *RusSec* sniffing around Tayside. Of course any of these multinationals could come in with a loss leader and snap up Strathclyde. He was only too aware of that.

He smoked a small cigar as he studied the print-out at the bottom of the pile with interest. It was from Cormack. It just said – *Lucini? Give me a call.* He didn't want to call, not trusting the Brigade's Integrated Communication System, at least not for anything sensitive. *It's all on BICS these days* he'd be told and that was just what he worried about. Anyone determined enough could hack the system, or pay someone to do it. Even encrypted messages were vulnerable. He asked Moira, his PA, to arrange a meet-up with Cormack in the usual place.

Daid felt he'd done enough for the day. He called for his car and took the lift to the basement car park. His driver opened the front passenger door and Daid sank into the soft leather rear seat. As the vehicle purred up the ramp, he relaxed to the sounds of Madame Butterfly. The journey along priority lanes took only a few minutes. The car pulled off into a reserved Brigade parking bay and Daid stepped out and walked the short distance to a flower stall. He looked carefully through the potted plants, fingering them, prodding the peaty soil. He selected an azalea, paid for it and then crossed the road to the embankment.

Cormack was in his early forties, a big man with surprisingly small feet. His neatly trimmed moustache gave him the look of a louche black and white film star.

"Is it arranged?" Daid asked.

"Yes. It went fine."

"That's good. What about the partner?"

"She knows. I told her."

"You did? Was that wise?"

"It's OK. You don't need to know the detail."

"What about the parents?"

"Well, we've got a bit of a complication there. Sergeant Major Garside was a little delayed getting to them. By the time he did, he discovered that the man who found the body had beaten him to it – must have been on some kind of sympathy trip. I can only guess that one of our people must have leaked the parents' address. We don't know who yet or why? This guy's from the Outlands, a forester I think, active up till about ten years ago, but quiet since. Lucini's parents are harmless enough, old man's gaga, the mother's a bit simple. But she told our man that she'd had quite a long conversation with the forester about her daughter. He might be poking around. I'll have to keep an eye on him."

Daid gazed at the river traffic and his mind drifted off momentarily. A sudden blast from a ship's hooter brought him back to the present.

"What's his name – this forester?"

"I've got it here somewhere," Cormack said, shuffling through his papers. "It's Landsman – Ellis Landsman." Daid went quiet and a little pale.

"Are you sure?" he asked. Cormack nodded and wondered why his boss was taking such an interest.

"Damn. He could be trouble. I knew his father."

Daid thought about John Linwood. He'd been a clever man, a man of principles, the wrong principles of course, but he'd respected them. The local Brig boys had just treated him like any other awkward politico, roughed him up, fitted him up and then locked him up. He'd only lasted a few weeks. He'd had influential connections and there'd been an almighty stink. Carpets had been rolled back revealing a range of unsavoury items. Daid owed his own promotion to the investigation. His predecessor as Commander had carried the can for the 'systemic failures' as they'd been described. Daid was the so-called new broom, not that anyone wanted any real sweeping done. He'd met Linwood just the once, interviewed him without overstepping the mark. In other circumstances he felt he could have enjoyed a philosophical discussion with the man.

He wondered whether Ellis Landsman had inherited his father's inquisitive instincts and his determination.

Cormack looked annoyed. "Is there a problem?"

"Well there could be." Daid rubbed his chin. "But on the other hand I can't imagine him getting very far. If we go in heavy on him, he'll smell a rat and that might make him more determined. So, keep a check on him by all means, but tread carefully. Of course if he crosses any real boundaries you'll have to stop him. Can you see a downside?"

Cormack could always see a downside, but he just shook his head. He could tell from the way his boss was looking at him, that gleam in his eyes, that he didn't want to hear anything negative.

"Are you racing?" Daid asked. Cormack nodded. "Good man – see you there."

Cormack walked away along the embankment, hands in pockets, head down. Daid didn't particularly warm to him, but he was very efficient. The Commander spoke into his mobile and within seconds, his car arrived and they sped off.

The arrival of the Shanghai Coupe X triggered the opening of the gates to the upmarket riverside community. Daid picked up his briefcase, which contained nothing of importance and stepped from the car and through the front door of his villa. The development had been built on land which had previously been a public park and was tree-lined and lavishly landscaped. There was a residents' bar with a patio overlooking the Clyde.

Within minutes of arriving, Daid had changed into chinos, deck shoes, a pale grey shirt open at the neck and a light fleece and had walked through the covered way to the bar, to sample their new consignment of Rioja. The place was already half full of residents and their visitors. He sat in front of the large picture window in a well-cushioned cane chair sipping his wine and sampling the tapas distributed in small bowls in front of him.

"Good to see you Charlie." It was Gregory Pelham, a man in his early sixties, though he looked older, with a goatee beard and rimless spectacles. He looked rather too much the part – the top man in a shadowy secret service organisation, SecureScotland.

"We need a quick word before you get too relaxed."

Daid gestured to the empty chair beside him. He didn't like his boss, didn't trust him – never had done. But he forced a smile and offered his guest a plate so he could sample the Spanish savouries.

"It's a little delicate really," Pelham continued, stroking his beard with his right hand then fastidiously cleaning the fingers of his left hand with a serviette. "It's your performance stats, not really up to scratch. I may have to send a note through to London – tricky time of course with contract renewal in full swing!"

Daid hadn't expected this. The figures were down but not significantly. What was Pelham really after? He resented having to haul his mind back into work mode. He mumbled something noncommittal and said he'd check the detail.

Pelham looked pleased. He'd caught Daid without an answer. He carefully placed a sliver of whitebait in his mouth and waved dismissively at Daid as he walked away to speak to the steward.

Daid had lost his laid-back feeling. Bloody Pelham! He knew his timing had been deliberate. He consoled himself with the thought that he'd be seeing Tanny later that evening.

+ + +

As Colette reversed the Transit into the lock-up and retrieved the simulator, Gam reflected on their trip up north. It really had been a waste of time and fuel. He'd have to forget the idea of a feature on Meikle. The man was a danger to the opposition movement and Gam wondered whether he should expose him. They walked slowly back to the flat.

The chaos they'd left behind the previous day was there to greet them. Reluctantly they set to, cleaning, tidying, repairing where possible and cursing. It was only when he was about to leave the flat with two full rubbish bags that Gam noticed the small piece of paper squashed up against the door jamb. He picked it up, smoothed it as best he could and studied it. He wasn't sure what to make of it. Was this part of a Brig trap or just some kids having fun? He showed it to Colette. She didn't see any harm in ringing the number. They could do it once they'd finished the clean-up.

As he worked away, Gam kept seeing a face in front of him, Kilbride's face, Meikle's number two. He knew he'd seen the face before, but it seemed like years ago. There was something oddly distinctive about it. Perhaps it was his eyes, slightly too close together.

They succeeded in getting the place reasonably habitable, made a pot of tea and some toast and sat on the sofa, drained of energy. At least the sofa was stable. The Brig boys had succeeded in snapping one of its small legs in their recent rampage but Colette had managed to fashion a repair of sorts.

Gam called the number of their unknown visitor. All he got was an answerphone which referred to some forest products company. He saw no point in leaving a message. Obviously a mistake or a wind-up and they had no particular need for forest products in the middle of the city.

He retrieved his second laptop from its hiding place under a false panel inside the dishwasher. They never used the machine, but left it looking like it had been recently in action, a few soap suds scattered about, some dregs of food waste attractively decorating the bottom of the washer.

He set about constructing the new website, with sections dealing with banking, energy, national government, security and fun. The site was used as notice board and carried limited information which was changed frequently. There were links to various social media sites, in particular *Any Change Pal* which was used by activists. Users were adept at leaving false trails and at using code and slang which changed before snoopers could get used to it.

When the mobile rang, Colette took the call. The voice at the other end was cautious.

"My name's Ellis. I think you may have just called my phone. Did you get my number from a note pushed under your door by any chance?" Colette confirmed this was the case and asked the caller what he wanted.

"Well, the thing is, I've not got much to go on." He made a highly censored reference to Carla's death and then talked about his visit to her parents and the limited scraps of information they'd given him. When he started talking about bumping into their near neighbour, he realised he was sounding increasingly unconvincing. But he ploughed on and completed his tale.

"So, what do you want from us?" Colette spoke hesitantly.

"I'd like to try and find out a little more about this Carla Lucini. Does her name ring a bell?"

"No, it doesn't, but then so many people have changed their names these days to escape something or other. Mind you, there must be other Gordons with ginger hair living in this neck of the woods. But, why don't we meet up anyway?"

Colette had taken an instinctive decision about the caller. He sounded OK, a bit odd perhaps, but not a risk. They agreed to meet the following day at the Botanical Gardens. She finished the call and turned to Gam who'd had been listening to one end of the conversation with increasing curiosity and frustration.

"You could have asked me before agreeing to meet this oddball." He sounded peevish and she told him as much.

"You trust me with slightly bigger decisions every day. I don't think a twenty minute chat under the palm trees is going to compromise anything." Gam felt suitably chastened.

It was only later, as he was dropping off to sleep, that Gam saw Kilbride's face in another context. The figure floating in front of his eyes was wearing Brigade fatigues, a younger man, but the same features. Then Gam remembered. He'd been in a car, unseen, watching the man as he'd arrested a demonstrator, a close friend of Gam's. He'd thought about intervening, but had known it would have been pointless and dangerous. It must have been at least five years ago. So, Kilbride was undercover now! No wonder he'd seemed somewhat out of place. Gam thought maybe he could run an article on Meikle's gang after all, only with a rather different slant.

*November 27th

I've made a decision – time to restart the diary. There's a lot happening that I don't want to forget.

Well – what a day! It started badly, but that's not unusual these days. Mortenson's such a git – a typical testosterone-filled man. But, I'm the one who chose this line of work, so I'm always going to get more than my fair share of idiots. As Aran says at her most sympathetic – I've only got myself to blame. But when I think of my induction, all those years ago – that nice man in the charcoal-grey suit and silver tie, with his highly polished shoes and not a hair out of place, how did I end up with a slob like M?

Anyway he told me to use my cover to get the detail on the plans for the New Year's Day action – the N weapons one. Apparently the organisers reckon they'll be able to take advantage of the collective hangover in the security biz that day and surprise us all. I think it'll be a damp squib but try telling M that. So I put my best Eco-Action hat on this morning and set off for the far east. Callan had told me about this anarchist collective in Fife. I thought it was the start of one of his jokes but he was serious. Not my patch, so I'm not familiar with the set-up.

Normally I like the cat and mouse stuff. Most of the 'opposition', are so amateurish, we run rings round them. But the trouble with the N weapons lot is that I agree with them by and large. And the last thing they are is terrorists. (I can hear Aran telling me to stick to my job and not get woolly minded.)

I did a bit of digging around and came up with three main

organisers. One of them sounds hardcore and has actually served time for various offences including criminal damage and assault. So of course I had to meet him. He calls himself Lemmy.

We met up in this dingy café in Pittenweem on the Fife coast with the wind blowing a gale. I have to say our Lemmy is a bit of a hunk, not at all what I expected. We had a quick cup of tea, and then he suggested we went for a walk – less chance of eavesdropping and all that. We got the boring details out of the way but I could tell that he didn't really believe my cover story. Normally I'm very good at this. I've always liked amateur dramatics and can play a part without giving the game away. But it was as if he could see though my disguise. But then I'm not sure about him either. He's very quick and very perceptive. Maybe I'm maligning the anarchist profession but he didn't seem at all like one. He began to make me feel a bit uncomfortable, a bit exposed.

Suddenly he came out with it and told me I wasn't quite what I said I was. The wind was really strong – we were on the harbour wall and I played for time by pretending I hadn't heard him. The spray was blowing across the quayside and we both got soaked. I told him he made a pretty unconvincing anarchist and he said that was deliberate.

Lemmy led me to this shelter at the end of the jetty. It was the kind of place courting couples would have gone in the old days. He was definitely getting to me and under different circumstances I might have done something about it. (Ignore this bit Aran.)

I really wasn't expecting the information he came out with. It was like a switch had been thrown somewhere in his head. I remember him wiping the spray from his face with a checked handkerchief. He told me how he'd been fitted up a few times before. The last time, which had been about six months ago, he'd been interviewed by the Brig as usual. But then they'd brought in D17. They'd found some stuff on his laptop which he'd forgotten to wipe, careless really, all about

nuclear weapons and the threat to reopen the mothballed base at Skroda Point. Well they weren't at all friendly. He told me he'd been kept in their place down near the Barras for 48 hours. They'd seemed a bit spooked. Part way through the interviewing process, when Lemmy had been hanging over the side of his chair, having just thrown up over the floor, a man had come into the room carrying a clipboard, down at his side. They'd thought Lemmy was out of it, which he pretty well was. But his eyes were still functioning OK. He saw this sheet of paper on the clipboard and the words 'private and confidential' in big bold type, followed by the word "Darkstone". He said he only remembered the name because he thought it sounded quite poetic. In the end they let him go.

He wouldn't have thought any more about it, but a few weeks later one of his guys had been arrested after a demo at Polshore Power Station. He got the D17 treatment as well but they must have gone too far. He had a dickie heart and he couldn't cope with the threats against his family. When they'd released his belongings, his wife had found a tiny ball of paper stuck in his trouser pocket, which the Brig had missed in their pre-release search. There was a single word on the paper – 'Darkstone.' She had no idea what it meant but had told Lemmy about it.

We'd got a bit cold and damp while he was telling me all this, so we walked back along the harbour wall. There was this group of teenagers on the beach throwing rocks into these huge waves. They didn't seem bothered by the spray. Some of them only had t-shirts on.

I asked Lemmy why he'd told me his tale and he said it was just something about me. He thought I might have the same views as him – whatever they were! We ate chips in the fish and chip cabin and stared out at the breakers. He said he'd be doing some digging around to find out more about Darkstone.

I'm not sure about him. Something doesn't ring true. Of course

it could just be a test – bloody Mortenson looking to see where I take this information. In which case Lemmy could even be one of us.

He didn't look back when he left – just walked off into the darkness. Aran says I should ignore it – told me not to get involved. I wonder.

December 5th

The wolf was not the leader he had been. The pack had been forced further and further south in their search for food. His reactions were slowing, his once lustrous coat was dull and mangy and he sensed he would be challenged soon. They'd found an abandoned sheepfold which gave them shelter from the wind and the snow.

He padded alone over the open moorland towards the long line of fencing in the distance. He reached it and followed its curve uphill towards the reservoir. The concrete posts stood like sentinels giving the fence strength and purpose.

He picked up the clear scent on the breeze. Deer were close by, which drove him on. He eyed the fence carefully looking for a way in, but it was sturdy and well built. Then he saw the change in the land. Where the fence climbed a steep hillock, the ground on the inner side had given way, weakened by weeks of rain and then snow. There was room for him to sneak under. His mood brightened, maybe he was onto something. He broke into a trot, following the scent as it strengthened. He saw the muntjacks about twenty yards ahead, in amongst the saplings. He was downwind from them giving him the advantage. He moved quietly towards them. The one on the left was smaller and probably slower. He sprinted the last few yards, catching the creature by surprise. The kill was easier than he'd thought, going for the back legs, to bring the young deer down and then a single bite to the neck. The creature was too big to drag back to the fence.

Despite his hunger, he left, retraced his steps and returned to the sheepfold. He attracted the attention of the rest of the pack and they set off at a canter. They reached the young deer and tore at the raw flesh, snapping at each other periodically. Their leader was alert. He didn't like being the wrong side of the fence and began to chivvy them to finish. They needed to leave.

He heard the breaking twigs first and then voices nearby. He warned the pack and they sped away through the trees, towards the fence. The gap was small and took a little time to negotiate. He was the last one through. As he struggled up the hillock on the opposite side, he felt a sharp pain in his back leg. He left an incriminating trail in the crisp snow as he limped after his comrades.

The wardens surveyed the hole beneath the fence.

"Let's get this fixed first, otherwise we'll have more of those bastards in here. We can track down the one we winged later."

The speaker radioed in to Base and ordered the 4x4 and the tools. They sat by the fence, smoking, cursing how their job was made all the harder by the protection wolves still had. Poachers were bad enough but at least there weren't many of them now.

"We'll be able to do him if we catch him. It'll be a Section 4, like that albino one we got last year."

His taciturn partner just nodded and stubbed his cigarette out in the snow. He hated the job, endless hours of boredom punctuated with brief moments of action and the very occasional chance to use his gun. He was all for following the wolf immediately, but his partner said they should wait for the vehicle.

Lucas hadn't made it back to the fold. The pain had become unbearable. He'd tried to continue, half walking and half dragging himself across the snow, but, exhausted, he had fallen to the ground. He was only half conscious of the vehicle when it pulled up beside him. He wasn't in a position to threaten anyone and he didn't imagine the pack would be returning to help. He could see the boots in front of his snout and heard a voice. It sounded reassuring. He made an effort to bare his fangs when he saw hands reaching out to lift him from the ground, but couldn't move. He could feel himself being shaken as the vehicle moved slowly forward. He smelt another creature although there was no sign of one. He drifted off.

Once he reached the house, Ellis shut Laska in the kitchen and then lifted the wolf out from the back of the Land Rover. He didn't resist at all, just kept a watchful eye open. Ellis took him to one of the outhouses. Laska was barking furiously, but Ellis ignored him. He rummaged in the metal trunk and retrieved a syringe and a capsule. He didn't want to find his wolf regaining consciousness half-way through his attempts to clean the wound. He injected the anaesthetic, just as he did from time to time with the sheep.

Lucas was spread out on the workbench. The blood had begun to congeal in the cold, but smears covered the wooden surface and the metal vice that was fixed to the front of the worktop. Ellis examined the wound. Luckily the bullet seemed to have passed straight through the flesh. It had caused only limited damage and the bone was still intact. He doused the wound in disinfectant and taped a bandage on as strongly as he could. He'd been in two minds as to whether to use a bandage, but the wound was still raw and he was worried about infection. Job completed, he loaded the wolf back into the Land Rover and set off for the hillside.

When he reached the place where he'd found Lucas, he placed the comatose body onto the snow. There was a risk that he might be attacked whilst still out cold, or that the deer farm wardens would track him down and kill him as they'd be entitled to do. But the longer the wolf spent with him, the more likely the rest of the pack – if he had one – would reject him. Ellis took a last glance at the prone figure through his wing mirror as the vehicle climbed slowly back towards the house, over the uneven ground.

+ + +

Ellis had barely had time to wash the wolf blood from his hands and change his soiled shirt and trousers, before he and Laska made the journey to the Glasgow botanical gardens, by Land Rover, train and subway. He still managed to arrive early as intended. He studied the huge palms, breathed in the warm, moist, earthy atmosphere and bit into the apple he'd brought from home.

The gardens were still open throughout the year, despite the heating costs over the winter months. They'd installed solar panels after a public outcry about its threatened closure

Ellis saw the couple arriving. Their images were distorted through the imperfections of the greenhouse glass. It reminded him of a visit long ago to the fairground, laughing himself stupid at the funny mirrors. His father had taken him there in the days when he'd had time for that kind of thing. His mother was already seriously ill. He could picture her waving them off from the living room window, a blanket draped around her shoulders.

Colette did the introductions. Ellis looked puzzled when she called her partner Gam. She explained it was a nickname made up from his initials – Gordon Alistair Mossman. Anyone that knew him well just called him Gam.

They made their way to the garden café where, luckily, the dog was allowed in. They ordered hot chocolate, a real luxury and toasted teacakes. Ellis noticed a group of old men sitting outside on the park bench, scarves wound tightly round their necks, caps pulled down low, breath streaming upwards in the crisp, cold air. One of them seemed to be telling a joke and when he reached the punchline, the other two dutifully broke into smiles.

Ellis told his story, leaving out very little. Gam and Colette listened patiently. She patted the dog as he lay quietly under the table. They said they didn't know anyone called Carla, but that maybe she operated under more than one name. Ellis thought about the picture he had of Carla's face on his phone. It was blurred and oddly lit in the torchlight. He considered showing it to Colette but decided against it. He wanted to keep her onside. A vision of Carla lying in her shallow grave might be just the thing to drive his guests away.

Colette stared up at the glazed roof for a long while as if some memory was stored there. She started talking rather suddenly.

"I've just had a thought. There was this woman who came to see us. There was something worrying her, something big. But she wouldn't tell us what it was. It was very recently. I think she was trying to gauge whether she could trust us. I got the impression she worked in security but was having second thoughts about what she was doing. Perhaps that's why she didn't use her real name."

A fourth man had joined the trio on the bench outside. He was wearing a kilt, but the effect was somewhat spoiled by his bright red trainers and football top. The group trooped off towards the main road, jostling each other, clearly in high spirits.

"Mel! That's what she called herself. It was strange, because I didn't think she looked like a Mel. That might sound a daft thing to say, but I always try and match names to faces. And I remember now, you came in just as she was leaving, Gam. You'd been out on a job. It was a Saturday, so I wasn't at the college. She was cautious, but pleasant enough underneath it all. I told her about you," she said, looking at Gam, "but I referred to you as Gordon. That must have stuck in her mind."

"Is there anything else that you can remember about her, or

what she said?" Ellis asked. He realised that he didn't have a lot to go on, except the possible link to some part of the security service. He hadn't expected that kind of connection. It threw him.

"Not that I can remember." Colette paused. "Hang on a minute though, she did mention a man with a funny name. Lenny or Lemmy or something like that. She'd just met him and seemed quite taken with him – an anarchist living over in Fife somewhere."

"Thanks, that's really useful," Ellis said, wondering whether there was anything he'd be able to do with these random scraps of information. "By the way Gam, could I ask what kind of website work you do? Is it connected with security issues?"

Gam was reluctant to reply. He didn't know this man, didn't like the way he'd shown up. He wondered if this was all part of an elaborate Brig plan to trap him.

"To be frank, I don't really like to talk about my work. Some of the stuff is confidential and so I have to be careful." Gam knew this might sound over the top, but he didn't care.

"OK, that's fair enough," Ellis said. He could guess why Gam was being reticent. "How about a bit of a trade-off? I'll tell you something about myself and if you feel more confident about me after that, maybe you could tell me a little about what you do."

Gam agreed, although he could feel himself being sucked in and didn't really like it. Laska looked up from under the table. Ellis took a bottle of water and a small plastic bowl from his backpack and poured the dog a drink. Nobody in the café seemed to mind.

"I'm basically a forester," Ellis started off. "I do a few other things as well, like a bit of artwork and I keep a few chickens and sheep. I've not been involved in anything for years if you know what I mean."

Gam and Colette looked at each other and both nodded.

"The main reason for that is what happened to my father. I

don't really talk about this much. His name was John Linwood."
He stopped to wait for a reaction.

"Shit – you can't be serious." The words were out of Gam's
mouth before he'd even thought about them. "Sorry mate! That
was a dumb thing to say. It's just that JL is up there with the greats.
He's an inspiration. How old were you when your father died?"

"Early twenties – so I knew all about what he was doing and
the dangers. I'd been involved in some of it, but luckily they didn't
pick me up. Afterwards I guess I just wanted to leave it all behind."
Ellis was finding it difficult to hold things together. He'd buried
all these thoughts for years, or at least tried to.

They got up to leave. The dog looked interested. Perhaps a
walk was in the offing. They set off around the gardens and then
down to the Kelvin. The river was in full spate and was dragging
down branches and whole tree trunks. An intrepid kayaker wound
his way skilfully around the debris, heading for the Clyde.

Gam told Ellis about the website, the zine and the kind of
activity they promoted. They talked about a possible feature on
Carla when and if they ever worked out what had really happened.
Colette walked the dog.

None of them noticed the man following at a distance.

+ + +

There was a sharp knock at the door. Gam had been asleep on the
sofa. It was dark outside and there were no lights on inside the flat.
He guessed it would be the Brig back for more. Reluctantly he
switched on the single low power bulb.

He was right. It was the same two as before, the man with the
shades and his sidekick. He was surprised they'd bothered to
knock rather than battering the door down. The man asked Gam
what he'd got for them. He was smoking a cigar. He hadn't asked,

just lit up, flicking ash onto the floor when the mood took him. The flat was cold. They'd run short of gas units for the month.

"Do you know about a man called Meikle?" Gam started off, knowing full well that they would.

"The name doesn't ring a bell but then one of my colleagues might know him. What about him?"

"He's dangerous. He leads a gang up in the hills. Here's the co-ordinates. He's planning something that'll cause damage – I don't know what. He's armed. Maybe not all his weapons are up to date, but he has plenty of them."

"How do I know you're not just making this up?" The man was trying to stop himself from looking interested.

"You don't. But I'd be taking a stupid risk to try and con you again." Gam was referring to a previous occasion, a few months ago when he'd fabricated some information and paid the price for it.

"OK, so why've you volunteered this information? Surely this man's an ally of yours, isn't he?"

"Look – as I've told you time and again, we're not into violence. I don't know why you never listen. Meikle's a danger, not just to his potential victims but to us." It felt strange sealing Meikle's fate. But his type of violent adventurism wasn't the way forward. He wondered how the Brigade would use his information.

His interviewer lit another cigar, using the glowing butt of the first and blew the smoke out across the room. Gam thought it was lucky Colette was out, not yet back from the college. She couldn't stand smoking in the flat and she'd have laid into the man with the shades, whatever the consequences.

"I'll check out your information. If it's duff, then we'll be back and we'll be taking in your lady friend as well. So let's hope for your sake that it stacks up. How did you get this information?"

"We went on a little trip. Your man lost us unfortunately." Gam couldn't resist the last comment even though he knew he might pay for it later. He wondered whether they'd check the Tracka records. There was nothing he could do about that now.

Once his visitor had gone, Gam waited a while and then retrieved his laptop. He prepared the story about Kilbride. After some diligent searching, he'd managed to find a photo of him on a curling website. He was apparently an accomplished player. He used this as the centrepiece of an article about Kilbride's forthcoming transfer from his current team to a destination as yet unknown. He didn't name his old team or its location. He wanted to keep the specifics to a minimum so that his fingerprints wouldn't be all over the article. He'd release it through 'Can of Worms,' a site used not just by politicos, but also by the celeb watchers. The beauty of this route lay in how difficult it was to track back to the originator. Gam lost himself in the intrigue.

+ + +

Colette looked at her watch. It was getting late. The two eighteen year olds slumped in the cheap plastic chairs were bright, but she was unsure which side of the legal fence they'd be, once they started using their undoubted entrepreneurial skills seriously. Like the other students, they'd been expelled from mainstream schools, after picking up a string of convictions and ended up in education rehab – the New Direction College as it was officially known. Colette brought the tutorial to an end.

She could see Tom Bairstow's outline through the frosted glass of the door. He came in as the two lads left.

"How's it going with them?" he asked, flicking idly through a car magazine that had been left on the table.

"OK," Colette said, suspicious about her boss' intervention. "Have you heard any more about those college grants." He ignored the question and asked her about Gam and what he'd been up to recently.

"What's happened?" she asked sharply. Tom was alright, but she knew the pressure he was under. All the teachers at the rehab centre were bolshie, non-conformists, involved in some sort of opposition. It came with the territory. He tried to keep them in line to protect the college's funding.

"It's the Brigade of course. They've just been down for another of their little chats. They always see this place as a hotbed of trouble, only this time they were nastier, threatening to get our funding cut. They're after Gam of course and they want me to use you to do it. To put it bluntly, they want me to fire you."

"And what will you do?" Colette was angry and nervous in equal measure. Apart from anything else, they needed her income. Gam earned next to nothing.

"I said I'd give you a warning. They weren't happy. But I'll speak to the boss – get in first. I think he'll be OK. I don't suppose you can do much about that partner of yours anyway. He is a bit intense though. Does he ever switch off?"

Colette mumbled something about commitment and then dried up. She asked Tom again about the Step Up course at the college. She didn't want to give up on the two lads.

"Depends on you really," he replied. "See if you can get Gam to lay off things for a while. I'll check with the college. Grants are scarce though. It's always tough. Are they off a Class Three?"

Colette couldn't believe it. This amounted to blackmail. But she wasn't really in a strong position.

"Yes. I'm worried that if we do nothing, they'll be running the estate in a few years – and not for the benefit of the residents."

"Names?"

"John Tollerson and Dominic Muir."

"OK."

She collected her coat from the staffroom and set off for home, more depressed than usual. The bus was one of the older ones. The driver sat stony-faced as she placed the exact fare into the plastic funnel. She climbed the stairs to the upper deck and rubbed at the misted-up window so that she could look out as they passed brightly-lit stores. The centre of the city had been spared the street-lighting axe. The shops were busy in the run up to Christmas, filled with glitzy baubles for those who had money to spend. As the bus moved away from the centre, the lights began to disappear and the shops became smaller and meaner, serving people with little to spend. She got off the bus at Partick Station and walked through the back streets to their block. Gam had told her frequently not to use this route, but it was quicker and Colette didn't take kindly to being told what to do. She walked slowly up to the sixth floor and let herself into the flat. The smell of stale cigar smoke that greeted her did nothing to improve her mood.

December 6th

It was only a short boat ride from his home, downstream, to the King George V Bridge in the centre of the city. Most passengers were in the over-heated lounge but Daid preferred the open deck at the back of the boat. Nobody else was braving the cold. He hung over the low rail. The air was biting. The spray flew away from the stern, seagulls examined the wake carefully, looking for anything edible and the twin exhausts of the catamaran gave a throaty roar which reverberated off the adjacent buildings. It was always an exhilarating start to the day. Daid waved to the pilot in his customary manner as he left the boat and set off for work. He stopped to pick up a take-away coffee from the stall by the bridge. He couldn't stand the stuff they served in the office. Mick who'd run the stall for years gave him the names of two horses running that afternoon at Ayr. Daid was a regular betting man and these tips paid off surprisingly often.

"So the going's OK today is it, Mick?"

"It's softened up just that bit, Mr Daid," Mick replied. He tucked a doughnut into a bag and handed it to Daid with his coffee.

Daid waited until he reached his desk before getting his caffeine fix and his intake of pleasurable fats. Moira his PA had placed his morning file on an antique table which stood to one side of the desk and he sat on the leather sofa to leaf through the contents. As usual, most of it was tittle-tattle. He made rapid progress.

He sipped the coffee and savoured each drop. He thought about Ellis Landsman. He could understand why he'd changed his surname, why he would have wanted to make a new start. He swallowed the last mouthful of doughnut and licked the sugar from his fingers. He noticed some of the correspondence he'd been leafing through was now stained with grease. Good – most of it was only worth wiping his fingers on anyway. He read the memo on Mossman and his woman. They seemed harmless enough, too earnest to be any real threat. He scribbled a comment on the paper and placed it in his out-tray.

When he checked his encrypted emails, the only one of interest was a piece of gossip from an informant of his within SecureScotland. One of their undercover agents, a guy called Kilbride, had been outed. The man must have got careless, but it happened every now and then – an occupational hazard. He'd be reassigned to a new area with some facial changes. They were trying to trace the source of the leak, but the information had been posted on one of those websites that was so convoluted that it made investigations very difficult. Daid wondered if he'd be able to use this information against Pelham in some way.

He got up to stretch his legs. Although he still played tennis regularly, he found he was stiffening up more than he used to. He'd need to see the club physio. He'd always prided himself on his fitness, from his school days when he'd fenced and rowed through to the army where he'd taken up squash and weights. As he stood in his familiar position by the window, Moira knocked and entered the room. She handed him a buff folder. She looked more serious than normal.

"You're not going to like it," she said as she left the room.

He sat back at his desk and opened the folder. It was the new contract of course. He'd been waiting for news. The e-memo on the top of the pile informed him that their bid for the next five-year Strathclyde contract had scored highly in the assessment process, but that *Great Wall* had a very similar score. He knew Chen, their top man, from his days in Hong Kong, when they'd made their own rules up. Now the rules were set by the commissioners in Edinburgh but all the strings were pulled from the Pyramid in London. Not for the first time, Daid cursed the success of the 'no' vote in the independence referendum. London interfered in anything that mattered but weren't to be seen if any of their schemes turned belly-up.

He consoled himself with the thought that at least he was still in the competition. He read on and groaned. He'd have to attend an interview with some bloody mandarin asking damn fool questions about things he didn't really understand. Perhaps he could just send his deputy? But no – that would be seen as a sign of weakness. The meeting was only a couple of days away. Moira had set up a briefing session for the following day. He noted that his boys were already digging around to see what dirt, if any, they could find on their competitors.

His phone rang. He didn't take many calls. Moira screened them all and normally came in to see him before putting anything through. He lifted the receiver. It was Pelham, one of the few callers who got straight through. Daid felt his morning was going to continue on its downhill trajectory.

"Daid, old chap." Pelham was as irritating as ever – couldn't even say hello in a normal way. "That business we spoke about the other day. We need to get together for another little chinwag. How about tomorrow evening 6:30, my apartment?"

Daid agreed. He knew he'd be in a lousy mood after the briefing meeting, but he wanted to get his "chinwag" with Pelham out of the way.

December 7th

The five horsemen moved slowly across the hilly, snow-covered ground. One of the riders galloped ahead of the group, dismounted and pulled a small video camera from his pocket. He caught his men silhouetted against the hillside, rifles slung across their shoulders, the barrels glinting in the sharp winter sunlight.

Meikle looked satisfied – it was just the right kind of shot. He'd post it when he got back to the farmhouse, anonymously of course. He'd been jolted by Kilbride's sudden disappearance and had considered calling the expedition off. But he'd invested too much in it and couldn't risk loss of face with the group.

As they reached the railway line, the snow started falling more heavily. They rounded the bend and cantered a little further, before stopping and tethering the horses to some saplings. They walked back, almost to the bend, struggling with the equipment.

Slug was small and muscular with thick, dark hair. He'd worked in the quarries until he'd been sacked for stealing explosives. He'd checked for the right location a couple of days earlier. Just beyond the bend in the track, the land rose steeply to the left. The abnormally wet autumn had left the ground waterlogged and unstable. Slug had calculated the optimum place to position the explosives to create the maximum damage.

He moved quickly with the fuse wire cradle and positioned himself under cover of some laurel bushes, close to the bend. His timing was deliberately tight in order to avoid giving any prior warning. The men crouched down behind the trees and passed round the hip flask. The cold began to penetrate.

Slug glanced at his watch. The train was late. He played a little game in his head as he always did when he was waiting for something. This time, he tried to recall the countries of Africa starting with Algeria and working round his mental map clockwise. He made progress down the East coast.

The driver looked out of the cab of the steam train and quickly withdrew his head. The swirling snow meant he could see very little. The fireman's face and lower arms were covered in a fine slurry of sweat and coal dust. He leant on his shovel for a while as they climbed the incline. In the brightly-lit carriages behind the engine, the members of the Entrepreneurs Club were enjoying their traditional, seasonal outing to Fort William. They'd finished the first course of pheasant terrine and were sitting back, swirling the dark red wine in their glasses and looking out at the wild world beyond the double glazed windows. It had been another successful year, a further wage freeze, corporation tax lower than anyone could remember and subsidised long-term loans.

No-one heard the muffled explosion or the dull thudding that accompanied the land slip. Their first realisation that something was wrong was when their carriage left the tracks and thundered down the embankment towards the river. The engine roared, as if in pain and hissed as it struck the water and the ground shook as it rolled over on its side. The carriages plunged into darkness.

From his hiding place, Meikle surveyed his handiwork. It had turned out even better than he'd hoped. He moved as quickly as he could with his camera, before lining his men up, overlooking the river. They fired a volley of shots over the crippled train, mounted the horses and rode slowly uphill.

The engine driver had been thrown from the cab on impact. He'd landed in thick snow which had broken his fall. He'd stared out at the surreal view in the distance, rifles, the sound of shots and then four or five men – he couldn't see clearly enough – riding slowly off into the distance. Later, when he'd been asked to describe the sequence of events, he couldn't be sure he hadn't imagined some of it. He'd told them about the bodies lying at strange angles in the snow. But his most vivid memory had been of the huge train wheels spinning in mid air and a sound like the engine was gasping for breath.

* November 30th

I couldn't put it off any longer – my home visit! I'd agreed with mother to stop for tea this time. Perhaps I should do it more often. I just wish I had something in common with them. They both seem so old – father particularly. Mother was her usual mock-cheery self, bustling around, clearing me a space amongst the usual debris, topping up my teacup, talking nineteen to the dozen and casting a wary glance every so often across to father in his chair. Where did their Italian spirit go? Perhaps they never had any. They've always been more like grandparents.

Maybe I do what I do now as a reaction against them. They're so staid, so boring – I need the action. Well that's what Aran says anyway.

Mother had dug out the three remaining cups and saucers from that floral pattern set we used to have. She'd even managed to find three matching plates. She loaded one of them with Battenberg cake and those little chocolate rolls covered in tinfoil wrapping. I used to love these. I still do, to be honest. Mother asked about my work. I told her the usual stuff about the websites and the magazines, about my workmates (invented of course). She asked, in a low voice, about my love life – as she always does. Of course I can't tell her about Aran. She wouldn't understand and father would go ballistic. I thought about mentioning "L." After all he is very nice. In fact I do fancy him. But then, I thought, the fewer people who know about him the better. I mean – who is he really? Is he really the activist he claims to be or is he just like me? I'll have to find out.

So I told her about Gordon – I mean we only passed each other in the doorway, but that Colette woman talked about him a bit, so I feel I almost know him. I told mother he has a bit of money, although judging by the state of their flat, they haven't got two pennies between them. I told her I'd been out with him, just the once so far and I could see her immediately thinking about wedding bells and all that rubbish. Still, it perked her up and it does no harm. She asked me about registration and I said that I don't need to re-register yet as my current address is still temporary. Of course the Brigade will know all about Aran at work. They'll have done the usual vetting.

When I went, there were the tears and hugs. I left mother the usual twenty pound notes, in the envelope, under the teapot. I wish she'd accept more. Father barely moved when I left, just a sort of grunt – about his only form of communication these days. I kissed him on the forehead. He was glued to some programme about polar bears.

It was a relief to jump into the taxi outside. The thought of walking through that estate in the dark gives me the creeps – me, with all my training. And it's not as if I can't afford the taxi. The driver droned on – moaning about every single road user, idiot pedestrians, the English and the Government. I tuned out and thought about father. He does seem to be losing it. Does he ever get out of that chair? Does he ever actually do anything? How does mother put up with him?

I got out just before Buchanan Street and walked the last bit. I tried to ignore all the Christmas gifts. But there was a wonderful display in one of the shop windows of these battery-powered puppets in winter costumes, singing and dancing. I could hardly drag myself away. As usual, I passed the workfare gang, standing huddled together in their orange uniforms, hunched over their shovels, smoking and spitting in rotation. God, they looked miserable. I

stepped into the peace and quiet of our foyer and the lift took me up smoothly to our front door. How nice it is here.

Aran was already back. She was sitting at the dining room table eating a sandwich and reading a book. Yes, an actual printed book. I immediately felt at home. It's probably the first time I've ever felt anywhere was home. I gave Aran a big hug. She looked surprised. She asked me how the parents were. I told her – just the same, just the bloody same as always. She asked me if I was alright – if I was still worrying about the Fife trip? I told her I was OK. She teased me about "L." I snuggled up to her on the sofa and gave her a kiss.

The phone call came completely out of the blue. Luckily I took it in the bedroom so Aran couldn't see or hear my response. It was the boss, Mortenson himself, about this undercover job I've just finished. Unusually for him he sounded really concerned.

My cover's been blown and M is seriously worried that they'll want to silence me. They're a real nasty bunch. M said I'll have to disappear for a while. I've got to go to this hotel and stay there until I get further word. Aran is used to me having sudden changes of plan so I didn't have to explain anything to her.

For the first time in this job I feel very threatened. If they find me, I don't fancy my chances. Aran's always telling me to be careful, not to take unnecessary risks, to remember that, at the end of the day, it's just a job. Well, it never has been and it certainly isn't now.

December 8th

The river flowed down towards Loch Airne. The waters were clear and icy cold. There was a stretch that ran close to the trees where it was a little warmer, a good spot for fishing, even at this time of year. The bright red berries on the holly trees stood out against the snow covered branches, looking like a photo for a particularly clichéd Christmas card.

Ellis sat on a folding, green, canvas chair with his fishing tackle box beside him. On top of this was a tray holding a variety of colourful metallic flies, glinting in the intermittent sunlight. Ellis balanced his half-eaten sandwich on top of the tray. He stared across at the copse on the opposite bank and reckoned he'd be able to start felling there before Christmas. He'd left the dog at home. He was just a nuisance when there were fish around.

Ellis selected a new fly and cast the rod, the line arcing out across the bend in the river. He sat calmly in the chair. Anyone observing would have assumed he was asleep, but he was in what he called stand-by mode.

Ellis sensed a presence. He knew straight away it was the wolf, Lucas, sitting on his haunches a few yards upstream, closer than he'd ever been before. He looked at Ellis and then at the rod as if he knew it was a potential source of food. Ellis noticed the blackened bandage on the wolf's back leg and wondered if he should try and remove it. He beckoned the wolf and to his surprise he moved closer. He reached for the scissors in his tackle box and encouraged the animal to move nearer still. He put some of the bacon from his sandwich onto the ground in front of him and waited. The wolf moved hesitantly towards the bacon and then snapped it up. He didn't move away but sat and then stretched out with his nose resting on his paws. Ellis decided against trying to cut the bandage off. It would drop off soon anyway. He replaced the scissors.

He'd rigged up a tiny bell on the rod and this began to tinkle. He had a bite. He reached for the rod and began to reel in rapidly. There was a flash of silver in the water. The trout was putting up a fight, it didn't want to leave its watery home. But Ellis was too well practised. He anticipated the fish's every move and held on. Eventually, exhausted, the trout gave up the uneven struggle and the water was still. All this time, the wolf had watched the action closely, unperturbed by the rapid movements.

Ellis used his gaff to land the trout, removed it from the hook, clubbed it swiftly and threw it across to where the wolf was sitting. He probably wasn't used to a fishy diet. But the wolf smelt it carefully and bit into it. It didn't take him long to get the taste.

Ellis chose a new fly and re-cast. The two of them again sat quietly watching the water. Ellis thought about the previous day and the long trip to Fife. He'd gone by train, first to Edinburgh and then on to Kirkcaldy. From there he'd caught a bus to Anstruther, just up the coast from Pittenweem. He'd been struck by the red pantile roofs. He'd taken a photograph of them so he could paint them later, roof after roof stretching away, with the sea beyond.

Tracking down the mysterious Lemmy hadn't been easy. To his surprise there'd been several anarchist groups in the area and he hadn't seemed to feature in any of them. People had been reluctant to give him any information and he'd had to call on Gam to get some doors opened. He'd eventually located his man and arranged to meet him on the harbour wall.

The sea had been calm which was unusual for December. Again Ellis had been obliged to refer to his father to establish his credentials. Lemmy had been visibly upset to hear about Carla's death and it was a while before the conversation moved on. Ellis talked about finding Carla's body and how he needed to discover what had happened. Lemmy had told him about the one occasion he'd met her and how he'd had this feeling that she wasn't really an eco-activist but that she'd been linked in some way to the security services and was working undercover but maybe in the process of going native. Ellis had made a mental note that this was the second time that someone had linked Carla to the security services.

What had particularly intrigued him was when Lemmy had referred to an undercover operation called Darkstone. Lemmy said he didn't know much about it but was worried that what little he'd told Carla might have led to her death in some way.

Ellis thought about his friend Ross and wondered whether to contact him again, try and find out some more about Carla. How should he play it? Maybe he'd just ask him a naïve question about whether Carla had been some sort of security officer and see what response he got.

The tinkling of the bell on the fishing rod brought Ellis back to the present. This time he was too slow and the trout slipped off the hook. The wolf looked on expectantly. He was clearly developing a taste for trout. Ellis recast and settled back.

When the sky began to darken, he decided to call it a day. He had four fish in his bag. He looked across to where his companion was sitting and threw one of the fish in his direction. The wolf caught it in his jaws and then trotted off up the hillside, without a backward glance.

As he walked back to Kintrawe House, Ellis felt his father's presence and asked him what he should do next.

"I think you should have another word with Ross. It can't do any

harm. Of course he may just clam up. But maybe it would be better not to mention this Darkstone project for the time being. It could compromise him."

Ellis was on his own again. He could see the thin trail of smoke from the house chimney as it spiralled slowly upwards. He knew something wasn't right as soon as he opened the front door. He'd left a pair of thick socks on the radiator to dry when he'd left the house earlier. The socks were actually labelled 'left' and 'right'. They'd been a joke present from Tora. He always put them on the radiator with the left on the left hand side and the right on the right. Always. But now they were hanging there the wrong way round. He couldn't hear the dog. He went through into the sitting room. He could just see Laska's back legs sticking out from behind the sofa.

✱ December 2ⁿᵈ

I really missed Aran's goodbye kiss this morning. I received this text summoning me to some place out in Mount Florida. They'd sent a car to the hotel which was very nice, but really I was shit-scared. I worried the whole journey that we might be intercepted. When I arrived I could see Hampden Park in the distance, the floodlights looking other-worldly in the daylight. I asked the driver why the lights were on, but he didn't respond.

The office building at Mount Florida is a clear contender for the demolition ball, flaking pebble dash, rusting metal windows, rutted car park. When I pushed open the outer door and looked into the dingy foyer, there was nobody else around apart from this odd looking man in a peaked cap sitting behind a worn reception desk that had seen better days. The man took me in the lift, down four floors. He didn't say a word, didn't smile. But I could feel him eyeing me up. The lift needed a good clean as well. He left me in this subterranean corridor. A woman arrived, just as I was beginning to get nervous and showed me into a small room with dim lighting.

There was a table pushed up against one of the walls and two chairs. The woman pulled a file out of her briefcase and stared straight at me. Her hair was tied back in a tight bun and she wore large glasses with big black frames. She wasn't in uniform which surprised me. She pushed this manila folder across the table towards me. I opened it and inside there were flight details and tickets, the name of a hotel in Antwerp and a new passport – my photo, but a new name. Apparently I'm now Janette Hammerton.

The woman told me they had a bag already packed for me and that I'd be driven straight to the airport. They had informed Aran and my parents that I'd be away for a good while. I'd have no contact with them or anyone else I knew. The woman had stared straight at me as she made these points. She said I'd be briefed on my new identity when I arrived in Antwerp. Why Antwerp? I've no idea. I was to go straight to the hotel. She gave me a final reminder of the likely consequences if I failed to keep incommunicado. It was all for my own good.

There was no chance to ask any questions. I picked up the holdall, put the passport and the tickets in my handbag and waited. The woman led me back up the lift and out to a waiting car. I could see the snow falling lightly in the glare of the distant floodlights.

The driver set off, turned on the musical wallpaper of Tartan Radio and closed the communicating panel between me and him. That suited me fine. I just stared out of the windows at the passing dreariness. Was it really necessary to have no contact with Aran? She'd be worried sick. Still as the woman said, it's for my own good.

I feel I've crossed a boundary over the last few days. My cover blown, doubts about what I'm doing and that talk with Lemmy was pretty unsettling. It's funny I've never really questioned the purpose of the jobs I've done before. I've just got on with them, I suppose because I've always felt we were doing the right thing. Improving security, fighting terrorism, it's for the benefit of all law-abiding folk isn't it? As the slogan says – we're Tackling Terrorism Together.

Now though, I'm suddenly not sure. We seem to have licence to do more and more as long as there's some sort of security justification. There are fewer checks or restraints. So far I've gone along with the party line, but I'm not sure how long I can keep this *up. Even legit opposition groups are being targeted and I keep falling over undercovers. I still think L might be one of those. Has he really been inside?*

But today's been real cloak and dagger stuff. What's next?

December 9th

"Charlie, take a pew!" Daid was in Gregory Pelham's overheated and over-stuffed penthouse apartment. He could see the river traffic and the bright lights of the city centre through the large window that dominated one side of the room. There'd been a big row when Pelham had first decided that, in addition to his Edinburgh apartment, he needed one in Glasgow. He'd bought an apartment in the development where Daid was already a resident. It was against policy for two senior security men to live in the same location. Pelham had tried to get Daid moved, but in the end, he'd managed to circumvent the rules and they'd established an uneasy truce.

"So you lost out to the Chinese, did you?" There was a look part way between a smirk and a wry smile on Pelham's face.

"Gregory, I'm surprised at you. You're normally so accurate with your gossip. You need to keep up to date. No, we've come to an amicable arrangement with *Great Wall*. We get a piece of Edinburgh and they get a piece of Strathclyde. It's called joint working. We've still to work out the details of course and we may just be stalling the inevitable, but it's better than I'd thought."

Pelham gave his *I know better* look which Daid ignored. He drained the contents of his wine glass and waited for his superior to refill it. There was an ivory mahjong set on the table in the corner of the room. Daid was certain the set was never actually used. He'd been a virtual addict of the game in his Hong Kong days.

Pelham walked across the room to fetch more wine. His wife entered the room carrying a tray of small Indian savouries. Daid thought she was the only good thing about Pelham. He could never work out whether Pelham knew. They'd been pretty discreet and Pelham sometimes missed the obvious.

"How nice to see you, Tanny." She smiled gave him a plate and held the tray in front of him. He chose an aubergine fritter. She walked with a slight limp, the result of a riding accident. She offered her husband the tray and then moved slowly to the door, smiling at Daid.

"Don't let Gregory talk you into anything will you?" Daid wasn't sure whether she was referring to something specific or just making her usual cautionary comment. She closed the door as she left the room.

"Well, what did you want, Gregory? I'm sure you didn't bring me here just for the small talk. No doubt the Pyramid are after something." Daid knew from long experience that most problems had their origins in the Pyramid, the London headquarters of SecureUK.

"Astute as ever, Charlie. Well it's the knock-on from the Kilbride business. Sorry, you won't know about this."

Daid gave the impression that he'd never heard of Kilbride and Pelham put him in the picture. "You see he was one of the Darkstone agents. Once he'd been outed he was no use for that operation. London wants an immediate replacement, someone who fits their bill, deep undercover, efficient, trustworthy, no awkward tendencies. You know the score. And on top of that they have another problem. Kilbride had a woman, worked on the data mining side of Darkstone. Totally against regulations of course, but Kilbride was like that apparently. So they have a sudden vacancy there as well. They've got nobody who's job-ready for either position, so they've asked me. And I'm asking you."

"Asking me what exactly, Gregory?"

"I should have thought that was obvious. Do try and keep up. I'm asking you to provide two agents who meet their spec. That's if you've got them of course. This is your opportunity, Charles. You wanted to run it remember?"

Daid remembered. The Pyramid had set up a high grade intelligence and provocation unit, operating on his patch, but under London's control. He'd fought hard to have it under his wing – but to no avail. London had been adamant that it was their shiny new toy.

"I'll get the agents," Daid said tersely, "and they'll meet the spec."

"Well make sure they do. We can't afford any cock-ups. Get their CVs to me within 48 hours. I'll inform London."

Daid thought this was typical of Pelham. He wanted to control the whole process, in particular the access to London. And everything had to happen yesterday.

"So, from what you say, Darkstone got a result with Meikle. Presumably Kilbride's job was to give him enough rope – before he got himself exposed of course."

Daid wondered, not for the first time, whether it was wise to make such comments in Pelham's flat. He always felt that nothing was off the record with Pelham. He had no actual evidence, but he thought Pelham was a bit of a Nixon – recorded everything for his own protection. He looked round the room speculating where the mikes could be hidden. They were so small these days that they could be anywhere.

"You're right, Charlie. Did you see those tabloid headlines – *Terror Deaths in the Snow*? It's given Darkstone carte-blanche really. They'll be rounding up whoever they want and issuing Stop Notices on the net like nobody's business. Now then, how about a few more of these delicious looking morsels?"

Daid sat for a few minutes longer, helping himself to the lamb pakora, one of his particular favourites.

"Well I must be off. I'll get you those CVs, Gregory. I must thank Tanny for her delicious snacks."

"You do that, Charlie. You do that."

Daid walked into the hallway and slid his arm around Tanny's waist. They kissed briefly.

"It's getting more difficult, Charles. I'm sure he knows. We should cool it at least for a while."

Daid agreed, a little too quickly for Tanny's liking. Not for the first time, she wondered who else he was screwing. She'd got used to watching other women watching him. Following her riding accident, she'd been unable to continue her dancing career and she was a little too hooked on Pelham's money. But she couldn't stand the man. Daid was a very welcome distraction.

Daid walked back to his own apartment. Having to put Tanny on hold was disappointing, but no more than that. He was intrigued by Pelham's request for two recruits. The more he thought about it the more convinced he was that he could use the situation to his own advantage, as long as he could identify the right people. With a couple of his own people on the inside, he could find out what was really happening. He'd heard a lot of rumours, but hard fact was difficult to come by. He'd have to be careful though. Those bastards in the Pyramid didn't miss much and they had a long reach.

He phoned Cormack.

+ + +

Iain Cormack was intrigued by the conversation he'd had with his boss. It was sensitive territory and their discussion had been carefully coded. He knew exactly which agents he'd be putting forward for the two posts. He'd inform Daid and then, once they got the go ahead, he'd control the whole process himself. Daid was not a details man. He'd tell him only what he needed to know.

He turned his attention to the report his man Garside had compiled on Ellis Landsman. He read that there'd been a meet up with Mossman and the woman. When Garside had broken into Landsman's house in the Outlands, he'd found nothing of any apparent interest there, apart from the name Ross and a telephone number scribbled on a scrap of paper. But when Garside had checked the number on the reverse directory, he'd found the phone was registered to Ross Lambert, a Brigade officer.

Cormack decided that the time had come to put an end to Landsman's little adventure as an amateur PI. He might become a danger. He summoned Lambert to his office. The man was clearly nervous. Cormack treated him coldly and asked him to explain why on earth Landsman would have details of Lambert's name and phone number in his possession. Lambert came clean immediately and confessed that Landsman had been a college friend and that for old time's sake he'd provided him with Lucini's contact details.

"After all, Landsman had found her body on his land," he added, trying to justify his actions.

Cormack went well over the top in his condemnation of Lambert and made threats of serious disciplinary action. But he stopped short of anything specific.

"Look Lambert, what I want you to do now is exploit your friendship with this man. His enquiries about Ms Lucini must cease. The body Landsman found on his land was not Ms Lucini. Her prints were matched to the wrong body."

Lambert was completely thrown by this information and took a while to absorb its implications.

Cormack explained that it had happened as a result of a clerk's carelessness, which had since been corrected. "So your job is to get him to track down the real owner, as it were, of the body he found. There are certain advantages to the Brigade in getting him to do this. And I've no need to emphasise that you have a vested interest in Landman's success in this little venture. Naturally you are to mention this to nobody – understood?" He handed Lambert a note with brief details about the real owner of the body and dismissed him from the room.

Ross Lambert felt like he'd got off lightly, but suspected there was much more to this than met the eye. Maybe it was all part of a bigger plan he was unaware of. He wondered what had really happened to Lucini?

He didn't know if he could convince Ellis to change tack. He could be very stubborn. But Ross was all too aware it was his own neck on the block. He'd have to be very persuasive.

+ + +

Ellis was wearing heavy boots, a helmet with a face mask and ear-protectors. The roar of the chainsaw shattered the tranquillity of the wooded valley. He dragged the smaller pieces of lumber to the trailer and used the horse to pull the larger ones. He'd borrowed the large grey from his neighbour Eric – his only remaining neighbour.

Taking a break, Ellis sat on a log to pour himself a cup of tea from a flask and roll a cigarette. He'd given up smoking years ago, but something about finding the body had restarted the habit. He blew smoke out across the small clearing, his bare right hand feeling the cold air, and thought about Laska.

When he'd seen the dog's lifeless form he'd feared the worst. But then he'd caught the whiff of chloroform and realised someone had wanted to immobilise him. Laska had taken a couple of hours to come round and was then shaky on his feet and kept bumping into the furniture. Nothing had appeared to be missing and apart from the socks, nothing was out of place, not even his laptop. They – he assumed it must be the Brigade – had been very professional.

As he sat on his newly-felled seat, he asked himself what was he doing playing the private eye? He was risking everything he'd built up and all for what – trying to find out why someone he'd never met had died. After all what could he really achieve? The figure sitting on the other end of the log looked across at him.

"You shouldn't be smoking those things you know" His father really knew how to get up his nose. *"And I don't think you should be throwing in the towel just yet. See what your friend says."*

"Well, that's if he is my friend. After the break-in I have my doubts."

"He was always a good friend." The figure faded away and Ellis felt the cold in his bones. He replaced his missing glove and picked up the chainsaw.

As things turned out he didn't have to make a decision. That evening he got a call from Ross. Ellis was in a bad mood, didn't really want to talk, but wouldn't say why. Ross eventually persuaded him to meet up. They agreed to meet outside the School of Art, an old rendezvous of theirs.

* December 3rd

I've walked here from the hotel. There's a huge barge ploughing upstream through the grey choppy waters of the Scheldt.

Well, what a strange 24 hours. This time yesterday, I broke the first rule. I know I shouldn't have done it, but I couldn't help myself. I found a callbox and tried to call Aran. A recorded message informed me that the number was no longer in use. It shook me, left me wondering what was going on.

Then I met up with my contact – C. A tall man, too much weight, distant, but didn't miss a thing. We walked from the hotel to a café just off the Grote Markt. The Glasgow snow has been replaced by Antwerp drizzle.

The Caffé Magritte is a bright, cheery little place and the coffee's actually affordable. We sat in a window seat. It was a good job I was actually sitting down when C started talking. He asked me how it felt to be officially dead. I assumed this was some sort of initiation game and played along. But then he showed me this picture on his phone. It was a dead woman, lying in the snow. She looked unreal. I have to say she didn't look anything like me although the picture was a bit blurry. I asked him what was going on and who the poor woman was? He told me to calm down. I already don't like him. He explained that the woman's death was a convenience which had allowed the old me to disappear and the new me to be created. It all seems coldly calculating but I suppose makes some kind of sense.

They aren't sure how she died – he thinks it was probably something drug-related. My new identity will mean I can escape my pursuers from that last dreadful job, so that's got to be a good thing. Can't help thinking about the woman in the photo though.

C told me my appearance would have to be 'adjusted' as he put it – hair, eye colour, teeth, face, even my skin tone. What they'll do to my face I've no idea. He said it would all take about a week, so I suppose I've got some kind of holiday. In the meantime he's off back to Glasgow and I'm stuck here.

* December 10th

The last week has really dragged, but I suppose it's all been necessary. My appearance has been 'adjusted' and the work doesn't seem to have left any scars. The facial changes are minor, but quite effective. I feel a different woman, probably because I am. For the first time in my life I'm blue-eyed and blonde-haired, with tanned skin rather than my usual sallow complexion. I've now got another new passport, with my new photo, but I'm still Janette Hammerton.

This time I met C in some anonymous office near the pedestrian tunnel under the river. No friendly cafes this time. He said I'd be working on another undercover operation. So far – so normal. Then he told me the name of the project – Darkstone. I couldn't believe it! When Lemmy had talked about it I hadn't known whether to believe him. It's suddenly become very real. I had to pretend of course that it was all new to me. I don't think I gave anything away. But I was apprehensive to say the least.

When C put some flesh on the bones and told me what my new role would actually be, it made a lot of sense. Apparently Darkstone is run from the Pyramid – now there's a surprise – although someone in SecureScotland has oversight of it – whatever that means. It all operates under the Tackling Terrorism Together umbrella. Basically anything goes, very few questions asked. The aim is to close down as many opposition groups as possible, using whatever means it takes. TTT gives us legal immunity on the grounds that it's all preventative stuff. The plan is that if it works well in Scotland, they'll use the same approach in England. As usual we're the bloody guinea pigs.

But the good news is that the top end of the Strathclyde Brig doesn't like Darkstone. My job will be to get the inside story, provide the incriminating details. This information will be used to undermine the operation and discredit it to such an extent it'll be closed down. C said they're against it because it's going too far, but I think it's maybe because the Strathclyde Brig doesn't have control over it.

Anyway, they're recruiting me to provide data for the undercover agents in the field. He said that I had needed a 'revised' CV, as he put it, to get the job and that my new identity had enabled that to happen. My old CV would not have been strong enough. So the fact that I've already got a brand new identity fits in perfectly. C told me that was one of the reasons I'd been selected for the job and also because apparently I've got the right mix of loyalty and scepticism! A complete loyalist would be no use.

There'll be two of us working indirectly for the Strathclyde Brigade – me on the inside and another agent on the outside, but we won't have any direct contact. This is strictly forbidden. Of course C wouldn't tell me who the outsider is. The less you know...

I asked C whether I had any choice about taking on this new role. He almost smiled. It didn't really suit him. He said he was certain I'd accept – hadn't really thought about the alternatives. His look seemed to suggest there weren't any. To be honest I'm up for it. It'll give me chance to escape the past, indulge my principles and get paid more for doing it. He told me I'd be starting work very soon which is good because I feel in limbo at the moment. I'm getting more and more worried about Aran though. What has she actually been told? And Mother. But then I'm always worried about her.

So I signed up – literally. The document was the usual bureaucratic mumbo jumbo but had a couple of key clauses about *not revealing my previous identity and not contacting any previous friends or associates over the next two months, without prior authorisation. This initial two month period is subject to extension – of course.*

I'm not sure about C. He's clearly Brig through and through and says the operation has backing at the top, but won't give me any more details. He's a cold fish but seems very efficient. I asked him about Aran – how had she been put in the picture? He told me he'd spoken to her himself. This was strange. He must be quite senior. Why hadn't he delegated the job? She'd had to sign a non-disclosure form. He wouldn't spell out what my mother had been told – just said that she knew what she needed to know. There was that assignment I'd had a few years ago when I was off her radar for several weeks, so it's not the first time for her that I've gone AWOL.

C gave me my return ticket and quite a large sum in cash – my credit card will take a bit longer. He told me how to keep him updated about progress in my new job and about the things I mustn't divulge to my new boss Major Morrisey. The operational base for Darkstone is somewhere under Central Station. C told me I wouldn't believe the number of tunnels and spaces underneath Glasgow. Certainly gives a new meaning to 'going underground'.

Finally managed to speak to Aran. She sounded different somehow. She confirmed that C himself had spoken to her and put her in the picture. She's the only one who knows – she must be trusted.

December 11th

The horses thundered down the final furlong, eyes staring, flanks covered in sweat, spittle streaming from their lips. The jockey on Ailsa Craig was using his whip to drive his mount to the finishing line. His shirt was chequered in white and purple which stood out against the muddy dull green of the track. His mount won by a head and as they entered the winner's enclosure, the jockey gave the briefest of smiles.

Daid looked at his race programme. He'd scribbled down the tips he'd been given by Mick at the coffee stall that morning. Ailsa Craig hadn't been one of them. He was going for Palomino in the next race at 5-1. He looked through his binoculars at the horses waiting in the paddock and spotted the number 7. The horse had done well at Chester the previous week. Daid adjusted his trilby. He always liked to dress the part and, from a more practical point of view, it kept his shaved head warm. His grey scarf was wound tightly around his neck and masked the lower part of his mouth.

"She's on board." Daid turned to look at Cormack's bulky figure. He was bareheaded and wore a long camel coat and brightly polished brown shoes.

"Yes, thanks for the message. Any problems?"

"She was a little confused to start with, but that's only natural. It's not every day you learn you're dead." A brief chuckle. "But she saw the sense in starting anew to escape the consequences of being outed in her last job. Not her fault, but the opposition are professionals, so she had to disappear. She's worried about her partner but that's just tough. She'll learn to live with it. She's the right choice."

Daid knew he could trust Cormack's judgement in these matters, even if he had his suspicions about him otherwise.

"What about the external?"

"He's grabbed the opportunity, not that I had any doubt he would. They'll complement each other. Not that they'll meet – we need to keep things in their separate compartments."

The horses were entering the starting gates, plumes of breath streaming out into the cold December air. They heard the starting gun and watched the ten horses as they disappeared towards the far side of the track. Daid pulled a chocolate bar from his pocket and offered a piece to Cormack, before stuffing two pieces into his own mouth. As the horses began to emerge from the mist, he reached again for his binoculars and followed his number 7 as it approached the grandstand. The horse was in third place and looked comfortable with two circuits to go. He glanced at Cormack.

"You got anything on this race?"

"Number 9, Smoked Salmond. Worse odds than yours."

The finish was close but Mick had been right. Palomino's timing was good, easing forward to clinch the race, with Cormack's horse a distant seventh. They walked across to the course-side bookies so that Daid could collect his winnings.

"How's Landsman doing?"

"He was in danger of becoming a nuisance, so I've arranged for one of my guys to meet him. Turns out they know each other from way back. I'm pretty sure that's how Lucini's address was leaked, but I can't prove it. This guy, Lambert, will pay Landsman a social call and warn him off the sensitive areas. He'll dangle some bait to send him off in another direction which will be useful to us. I'm confident Landsman will respond appropriately."

"What direction will that be?"

"Oh, just a back road."

Daid nodded. He didn't need to know the detail.

He handed his betting slip to a man sitting in a small cubicle, ruddy faced and seemingly oblivious to the cold. The smoke from his large cigar curled upward into the darkening sky. He took a swig from a small silver hip flask and handed the crumpled notes over to Daid. When he turned around, Cormack had disappeared, melted away into the crowd.

Daid lit his own cigar. He felt a touch on his elbow and was a little startled when he turned and found himself being confronted by Gregory Pelham. Before he had chance to speak Pelham was at him, his eyes red, hardly able to contain himself.

"You really are a bastard, Daid – right under my bloody nose as well. Well I'm not going to stand for it. You'd better watch your step and as for your performance figures…" He didn't finish the sentence, but turned and walked towards the car park.

+ + +

Ellis stood at the top of the steps outside the Glasgow School of Art, the students coming and going around him. The clock on the nearby insurance building struck six. He'd give it another quarter of an hour. He wondered how far Ross Lambert would want to go to help. He was already out on a limb which might be chopped off at any time.

He saw his friend in the distance making his way slowly up the hill. He looked tired, careworn, under the weather perhaps. Ellis vaguely remembered someone telling him that Ross had a young family. It couldn't be easy juggling his particular job with being a father. Still he was a grown-up – could make his own decisions.

But he needed to know which side Ross was on. Was he behind the break-in? He didn't think so, but couldn't be sure. He thought back to their student years. They'd both been after Tora and Ellis had won. Could Ross still be bearing some sort of grudge all these years later?

"Elly, how are you. Sorry I'm late, bloody underground. Let's get a drink."

They walked down Renfrew Street and turned onto Hope Street talking as they went.

"Look there's something I have to clear up straight away, Ross. Someone broke into my house, drugged my dog and searched the place. Tell me it wasn't you!"

Ross looked puzzled and affronted, angry even. "Shit! So they're on to you. I suppose it was only a question of time. Have you been aware of being tailed at all?" Ellis shook his head. "They can't know you got your information from me otherwise I'd have been shafted already – unless they're just stringing me along of course. But, no, it wasn't me. You'll have to take my word for that. If I'd been given the job – which could have happened – I'd have spoken to you first, asked you to leave the door open and I wouldn't have touched the dog. The thing you have to realise though, is that you've been acting like a PI. You can't blame the Brig for investigating you – especially with your background."

Ellis had to admit that Ross was talking sense. He'd stepped over a line and certain consequences were going to follow.

"How is your dog by the way – OK?" Ellis nodded. "Good. But, I think we've got a bigger problem. Look, I'm not sure about this but I think you're chasing the wrong body. Sorry – the right body but the wrong person."

Ellis stared at his friend. "You need to make a bit more sense than that. You haven't been drinking already have you?"

The pavement narrowed and Ellis stepped into the road

anxious to continue the conversation. There was a blast of a car horn and a throaty roar from a Subaru as it flashed past, the driver holding up two fingers out of the window. Ross said it would be easier to continue the conversation somewhere a little safer and led them into a small basement bar on one of the side streets near the station. He ordered pints and crisps. They sat by the window with a view of a grating above.

"OK. I've been trying to get some more information about Carla Lucini. When I went back to her records, I found access to her file history had been blocked. This does happen from time to time if something sensitive arises. I may be able to get round this but it'll take a while. So my only other way of getting information was through the body report and the fingerprint record. You remember I checked them that first day you contacted me when I came up with Lucini's details. When I checked the same body number again today it threw up a completely different name, someone called Rebecca Leuchars. I couldn't work it out to start with, but I realised that the morgue clerk must have got two bodies mixed up and then corrected the error, hoping nobody would notice. He'd have got away with it if I hadn't been so nosy."

"Wait, wait, wait!" Ellis was trying to control himself and finding it hard. " Are you're telling me I've been on a wild goose chase all this time, that the body wasn't Carla but was Rebecca someone or other. How can that be? Jesus – I told that poor old couple that I'd found their daughter's body – and now you're telling me it wasn't her it was someone else!"

"Yes – that's what I'm telling you – just calm down a little."

Ellis took a few deep breaths. He knew his friend was right, but he was really thrown by all this.

"So do you know anything about this Rebecca?"

"No, not much – name, address and ID number. When I've got time, I'll check what else might be available." Ross paused. He was trying to keep his story about Carla Lucini consistent. He didn't want Ellis to start speculating on what might really have happened to Carla.

Ellis felt like he'd been wasting his time. What was the point of him continuing to enquire about Carla, if she hadn't actually died on his land? He had no other link with her. But did he want to start again from scratch trying to find out what had happened to this Rebecca?

"The thing is Ellis, if someone has blocked access to Lucini's record it'll be because of some sensitive security issue. It could be dangerous for you to go digging around in these circumstances. But Rebecca Leuchars is really the one who needs your attention now. I know for a fact that the Brigade isn't making any enquiries about her death. According to the autopsy it was drug linked. If you don't follow this up, nobody else will. And, as we now know – it was her who was buried on your land!"

Ellis thought about this. It would be difficult to start again but perhaps he owed it to the woman. It might take him some time to rebuild his enthusiasm, but he didn't want to just drop everything. After all, in a strange way, it had given him a new lease of life.

"Let me have her last address and I'll give it a go." Ellis didn't exactly sound enthusiastic. Ross handed over the details.

"I really appreciate this, Ellis. If I come up with any more information about her I'll let you know." Ross could tell that that his friend was uneasy.

"But what about Carla's parents? I feel awful about them. Perhaps I should visit them again just to clear things up."

"No, no – I'll sort that out with them. You've done enough," Ross said. In reality he didn't intend to do anything. He had enough problems with Cormack already, without adding to them. And he'd no idea what the parents been told officially. "I'll get us another drink."

Ellis sat staring at the tiny Christmas tree in the corner of the room. It was an abject specimen, with half a dozen lights draped haphazardly across its already half-bare branches. There was a thin scattering of pine needles decorating the bare floor around the tree. He hadn't thought at all about Christmas or what to do over the holidays. Usually he took a few days off and spent them on a small island, where a friend had a croft. It was ironic, swapping the remoteness of Kintrawe House for the even greater remoteness of the Hebrides. He took a roll-up out of his tin and lit up. It was one of the smoking pubs that had recently been relicensed after pressure from the tobacco companies. Ross handed him a second pint and he drained half of it rapidly.

"So, I almost forgot. If you didn't break into my place, then who did?"

"That I don't know," said Ross. "I could hazard a guess. There's a guy called Garside who does a lot of that kind of work and I happen to know he doesn't like dogs, so he'd have come ready armed with something suitable. But whoever it was, don't forget the guy was only doing his job. I have to say it's pretty mild stuff compared with some of the things we get up to – not that I should be telling you this."

The elderly landlord shuffled into the room carrying a coal bucket. He put a match to the small pile of balled-up paper and kindling in the grate and then held a sheet of newspaper in front, to help the fire draw. There was a roar and the flames danced up the chimney. He removed the newspaper and piled several pieces of coal onto the fire, then stood back to admire his handiwork. They removed their coats.

"You gents be wanting a top up?"

"A couple of chasers would be good. Talisker thanks." The landlord moved slowly back to the bar.

"Look I'm really sorry about your dog. It's not the one you had when you were at college is it?"

"No, he went years ago. Laska's four, a Border Collie, at his peak really and great company. It's just been him and me since Tora left." Ellis stopped abruptly. "Sorry didn't mean to mention her. It didn't work out, my place was a little isolated for her to say the least."

"Don't be daft. I got over Tora years ago. I'm a family man now, two boys and the wife. Do you still hear from your dad by the way?"

"Regularly – especially at present. I find it strangely comforting. How about you?"

"Yes I'm the same. My ma always has good advice for me – even when I don't want any."

The two of them sipped the peaty drinks the landlord had delivered.

"So," Ellis said, "I'll see what I can dig up on Rebecca. Sorry – probably not the most appropriate phrase in the circumstances. What's the best way of getting in touch with you if I need to? I don't want to compromise you – well any more than I have so far."

"Probably best not to use the usual comms – too easily hacked. I'll set something up and let you know."

In the street, they shook hands and Ellis waited until his friend disappeared around the corner. He didn't feel like going home. Much to his surprise, he was getting to like spending time in the city. For some reason he suddenly thought of Lorna, the woman who lived a couple of floors down from Gam and Colette. He tried to remember what she looked like. There was something about her eyes. He'd found it difficult to look away.

He made his way to the underground and bought a ticket for Partick. As he stood waiting for the train, the smell of piss was almost overwhelming. The system was creaking at the seams. There was never enough money for repairs and trains were frequently cancelled. Anyone with a bit of money avoided it.

The sudden rush of warm air heralded the train's arrival. Ellis squeezed his way on and stood with his fellow sardines. The man facing him had a long straggly beard and hair to match. He had scratch marks on his cheeks and his eyes were dull and lifeless. He kept muttering about being shipwrecked. He chewed incessantly, looked as if he was tempted to spit, but thought the better of it. He carried a green plastic bag which had several newspapers and a bottle of milk protruding from the top. Every now and then he wiped his nose on the sleeve of his old tweed jacket.

The man also got off at Partick and stumbled along the narrow platform. Ellis kept his distance and emerged into the cold evening air. He tried to recall the route to the block where Lorna lived and had to retrace his steps several times before he got it right. He walked slowly up the four flights wondering if he should carry on or just turn round and go home. A voice in his head told him to go home but he ignored it. He knocked on the thick metal door wondering if anything would be heard on the other side of it.

He waited a while and was just about to turn and go when the door opened. She recognised him instantly and beckoned him to come in. Neither of them said a word. He removed his coat. She held him close to her and kissed him lightly on the lips. The voice again told him to go home, but for the first time in years he didn't want to be alone. He kissed her and she led him to the bedroom. It was too cold to undress properly so they got under the bedclothes and struggled to remove their clothing. It didn't really matter and they managed to entwine themselves sufficiently despite being still half-dressed. He couldn't recall the last time he'd been to bed with a woman – three years, four years?

It was the music that woke him – a thumping baseline from the flat above. He could hear someone clanking around in the kitchen and then saw Lorna carrying a tea tray into the room. She was wearing an oversized dressing gown, bedsocks and a woolly hat.

"I know how to turn a man on," she said, placing the tray on a rickety bedside table. "So, is Ellis your first name or your last name?" He explained and pulled her back into bed.

+ + +

He finished the last of the fry-up and pushed his chair away from the table. He'd managed to find his clothes, several of which had been inside out. Lorna sat looking at him from across the small kitchen table. He asked what she did for a living and she said she was a translator, a freelance.

"And what about yourself, Mr Landsman? What is it you do?"

He told her about the forest and the house. He suddenly found himself asking her if she'd like to come and see for herself. Where was this new impulsiveness coming from? She said she'd love to go. She'd pack a bag, make a couple of phone calls and they could be off.

December 11th

Ross Lambert reflected over the events of the past few days. It had been a strange unsettling time. He thought about his indecision when he'd taken that first phone call from Ellis Landsman. He'd had a premonition about being drawn into something he couldn't control. He'd been right. He'd hesitated long and hard about whether to go ahead and meet up with his old friend and hand over classified information – even if it was just a victim's name and address. It was partly a feeling of guilt that made him decide to go ahead. He'd always felt bad about what had happened to Ellis' father – even though it had all happened before he'd joined the Brigade.

Part of him wished he hadn't made that decision. He now found himself in deep and murky waters and he didn't want to face another grilling from Cormack. He was just relieved that no specific punishment had been dished out to him. That might come later of course.

Cormack obviously had his own agenda, one part of which was to prevent further enquiries about Lucini. There was something strange going on there. What he couldn't fathom was why the Major wanted Landsman to switch his attention to Leuchars. Why would Cormack be interested in her? What possible link could there be?

Ross knew he was in a vulnerable position. What he needed was some kind of bargaining chip, in case things got rougher. He'd have to do some digging of his own about Lucini, to try and find out what had really happened to her. It would be risky and he'd have to cover his tracks. Early in his Brigade career he'd spent time as a techie in the HR Department. He knew his way round the electronic records and, more importantly, he knew how to circumvent the security controls. He'd kept his hand in over the years, logging any security updates.

He used a public phone box to call to an old college friend, his technical guru. Between them they worked out how he might be able to pick the electronic lock on Lucini's file. He returned to the office and after a few false starts, gained access. He was surprised to find out that in addition to her registered address at her parents' house, she also had an unregistered address listed. It was tagged as "sanctioned," so it had official approval. This was unusual. He made a note of the address up near the Merchant City. The owner of the flat was Ms Aran Caulfield. With that address, she must have some money, he thought.

Having two addresses was irregular and he wondered what lay behind it. He replaced the electronic lock, removed his file access history and decided he'd pay Ms Caulfield a surprise visit.

He retrieved his bike from the underground car park and picked his way around the various street hazards, on his way to the Merchant City. The flat was easy enough to find. He locked the bike to a drainpipe, removed his helmet and stood outside the apartment block for a few minutes, realising that he hadn't really worked out what to say. *Is there a possibility that your flatmate might not be dead after all* didn't seem like the most subtle introduction he could use. He decided to play along with story that Carla was deceased. He pressed the button on the door entry phone. A woman's voice answered.

"Miss Caulfield. I've come to talk about Carla Lucini," was all he could think of saying.

"You'd better come up then," the disembodied voice said and the door clicked open. He ignored the lift and made his way up the thickly carpeted stairs. There were plants on each of the window sills, flourishing, well-watered plants, not the shrivelled, dying specimens that he was used to. He knocked on the front door of the flat and was conscious of being watched through the spy hole. The door was opened by a tall woman with short brown hair and piercing blue eyes. She gestured for him to come in.

He sat stiffly on the high backed chair. She remained silent and there was no offer of a drink.

"I'm afraid this is a little awkward," he started off tentatively. "I work for the Brigade and I've come to talk to you about your lodger, Ms Lucini. My condolences – you must have been shocked by her death."

"I certainly was." Her response was emotionless, not a trace of grief.

"I'm sorry to have to raise this issue in the current circumstances, but to tell you the truth I'm a little puzzled by something in our records. I understand that Carla was sanctioned to live here even though it wasn't her registered address. It's my job to investigate such anomalies and I wondered if you could help me out." Her eyes stared through him.

"And your name?"

"Sorry – Lambert, Sergeant Lambert."

"Well Sergeant, I know nothing of the inner workings of the Brigade. All I know is that Ms Lucini was a registered lodger here. I don't know why she was still listed at her parents' house. You'll have to ask your colleagues, won't you?"

He felt awkward. There was an almost tangible barrier between them. The flat was comfortable, warm, homely, in stark contrast to her manner.

"How well did you know Ms Lucini?" As soon as he asked the

question he realised it was a wrong move. The woman blinked momentarily and then rose from her seat.

"I don't think that's particularly relevant is it? I'm afraid I really can't help you Sergeant. If that's all, perhaps you could leave. I have some preparation to do for my work tomorrow." He wanted to ask her what she did, but thought that might be another inappropriate question.

"Well, thank you for your time."

As he descended the stairs, he replayed the conversation. The woman was hiding something obviously, but he had no idea what. He decided to find out a little more about Aran Caulfield.

December 12th

The last train had run through the old railway tunnel in 1921 and it had been abandoned ever since. The tunnel provided an emergency exit for the Darkstone base – not that it had ever been used. The base was located below an anonymous suite of offices overlooking the main concourse at Central Station. The offices were used by the SecureScotland Audit Service – a team which specialised in forensic work. Beneath them, the basement housed an old strong room used for storing confidential records and a key-access lift that took certain authorised personnel down a further two floors, to a bright, air-conditioned, open-plan office.

Major Irwin Morrisey, a dour, cheerless man waved his arm across the empty space.

"Of course, Charlesworth, this place is normally full of lasses carrying out our monitoring work. It's only empty whilst you're being inducted. As you know we've strict rules about the internals being kept apart from the externals. The women spend their time monitoring phone calls and social network sites and analysing the feed that comes from the SecureScotland email surveillance system. These days we're able to monitor content of course. These sources provide the raw material for our daily reports to you guys in the field – who's saying what, who's planning what and what's about to go critical."

Victor Charlesworth had spent most of his career working undercover, using the name Lemmy. The arrangements all seemed fairly routine to him, but he was interested in their ability to monitor content. He wondered quite why it was necessary for his boss to enforce such strict separation between the internal and external agents but supposed it was all part of a divide and rule strategy.

"You agents in the field use the information in these reports to assist our undercover work identifying and monitoring oppositionists so they can be closed down and brought in before they get completely out of control. Of course there'll be occasions when these people may need a little assistance to overstep the mark, in order to forestall future trouble, but you'll know all about that. And Darkstone has given our agents increased immunity to help them get the job done. All our externals are agents who've lived for years in undercover guises, creating new identities, forming long term relationships, having children and running businesses. I see from your CV that you fit the bill – even done time inside, I notice."

Morrisey looked at his new agent as if he didn't believe what he'd read. But Lemmy didn't rise to the bait. He'd taken an instant dislike to Morrisey and he could tell the feeling was mutual. Still he had a job to do and would need to establish a professional relationship with the man. Morrisey waited a while and then continued the briefing.

"What Darkstone has done is to bring this work under one umbrella, vastly improve the quality of information we're able to send out to agents, which in turn has increased their effectiveness. And we find, very helpfully, that the extent of our surveillance means that some miscreants choose not to use emails, or their phones or the internet, for fear of being compromised. Self-censorship saves us a lot of effort. As you'll be aware, Charlesworth, SecureScotland has notional oversight of our operations, but we're basically an arm of the Pyramid. The

Strathclyde boys wanted to get in on the act but they're not to be trusted. Being a Fifer, you won't know about Glasgow politics. But, take my word for it, Daid and his mob are on their way out.

"You'll have no need to set foot in this building again, by the way. All your information will come by encrypted link to your X20 wherever you're operating. We've had the machine custom built for our purposes and the encryption's first rate. We've never lost anything."

"How did the name Darkstone come about?"

"Oh, it was just computer generated, nothing more to it. That's about it Charlesworth, although I have to say, I'm curious about how you were recruited. I know it was a bit of a rush job to fill an unexpected vacancy. Who exactly was involved?"

Lemmy had been carefully briefed on this point by Major Cormack.

"You're right, it was a shortened process given the need for a quick replacement. But there was involvement from both SecureScotland and the Pyramid. I understand that's the way it's normally done." Morrisey looked sceptical.

Lemmy had always enjoyed his undercover work. He knew how to feed in the right kind of information to stimulate an appropriate response. When Major Cormack had approached him, through a common acquaintance, he'd jumped at the chance of joining the Darkstone team. Cormack had stressed that the most important part of the job would be his confidential, daily activity report on everything he came across, official and unofficial – the nature of the information he received, gossip about other agents, details about his SecureScotland handler. He'd been instructed to forward this report to Cormack alone.

Morrisey was in his 50's, a SecureScotland company man through and through, who expected complete loyalty from his subordinates. But he wasn't averse to bending or breaking the rules where necessary, if it meant securing their ultimate goal. His agents generally went along with this. They relished their freedom of operation and knew better than to rock the boat.

Morrisey instinctively didn't trust Charlesworth. He knew he hadn't been recruited to the team through the normal route. He'd been told by Colonel Pelham that London had wanted some fresh blood in the team, somebody with a suitably active track record. Charlesworth fitted the bill. Morrisey had to admit that his CV was impressive. He just didn't know how much of it – if any – was true.

* December 12th

Just completed my first day! Who would have thought that underneath the station, all that's going on? So far, no one has mentioned the word Darkstone – but then I didn't really expect to see it emblazoned in lights over the door.

The girls seem OK – a little suspicious at first, but fine when I told them about my (totally fictitious) track record. They call the place Spook Central, although its official name is Lawton House. The stuff that comes into the office is just amazing. I've done my daily log for C. Not that I had much to say from today's work, but I think that'll change quickly enough. I was analysing information from the email feed today which picks out keywords and then filters out suspect mails for a further series of tests to highlight the really interesting stuff. Except most of it isn't that interesting. At times, they (or should I say we) are scraping the bottom of the barrel – groups that would probably struggle to organise a car boot sale, let alone the overthrow of society as we know it. I can't believe what some idiots put into the system knowing that someone, somewhere, is trawling through their rubbish. Then again, some of the detail I saw today was at the other end of the spectrum. I'm not sure what controls there are on our agents in the field.

Apparently we don't get to meet them. It's all very sexist – us girls in the office and them guys out there. If I was here for real, I'd kick up a proper stink about it. But given my current status, it's just a question of keeping my head down. We're not allowed out during the shift (eight hours!) so we've got access to the kitchen, coffee on the go and all the ready meals we can eat. They're actually very good.

I really miss Aran. I'm very tempted to call round but I know I'm being monitored. Any false move would very soon become known and I'd be off the job, not to mention at risk of attack from the bastards I fell foul of in the previous job. As for the parents, at least they're used to me being out of touch, although two months will be pushing it.

The thing I'm really worried about is who is authorising my work – I mean there must be someone above C? I don't want to find myself completely out on a limb if anything goes wrong. I've got no hard evidence to show an investigator if they ask me any difficult questions. So that's why I spoke to Val, my legal guy, a civilian. He's taken a sworn statement from me – which I'll add to now and then – and I've given him a few bits of hard copy documentation I picked up from my induction. It's not a lot, but better than nothing. Maybe I'm just worrying too much.

On the other hand if it all goes well, this job will be good for my CV. And of course it's the right thing to be doing.

December 13th

Even though it was 8:30 it was barely light. Ross Lambert stood under cover in the doorway of a disused shop his eyes glued on the entrance to the smart-looking apartment block on the opposite side of the street. It was past nine by the time Aran Caulfield came out of the entrance and walked briskly away. Ross was frozen. He managed to get his limbs working and followed her at a safe distance.

They boarded a suburban train going towards Bearsden. His Glasgow day pass had been a good purchase – no risk of losing her in the crowd while he tried to buy a ticket. After the first few miles of semi-dereliction, the suburbs started to look prosperous, with a series of gated communities, parkland and streets with up-market shops and bars. That was the thing, Ross thought, two very separate worlds and the longer current policies continued, the less contact there'd be between them. The better-off had no reason to set foot on the Estates, they used private healthcare and private education, the main roads to town were well-maintained, they were well paid, inflation was low, house prices were increasing again after years in the doldrums and domestic help had never been cheaper. Flip the coin and the poor seldom left their Estates, food and heating were costly, public services were poor or non-existent, whilst for anyone lucky enough to find work, wages were low and jobs insecure and often only part-time. The only thing that was cheap was the booze.

Aran Caulfield picked up her bags and left the train. Ross had been staring out of the window and almost missed her. He just made it on to the platform before the train doors slammed shut and the train accelerated away. She stopped to buy a magazine at the stall and exchanged a few words with the vendor, an old woman who looked to be well into her eighties. Ross followed slowly, bought a packet of chewing gum and pushed a stick into his mouth. He followed Caulfield as she descended the steps to the street below. Within seconds she'd sprinted across the road and boarded a city-bound tram. Ross stood rooted to the spot feeling like a complete amateur.

There was no point in trying to follow. She'd obviously spotted him. But he hadn't been that careless – she must be some kind of pro. At least, if that was the case, there'd be other searches he could carry out on the Brigade system to get more information about her.

There was a breakfast bar on the station platform which looked inviting. He decided he could stretch to a coffee. He could stick it on expenses. It went nicely with a roll and sausage. He exchanged a few words with the man behind the counter. 'Barista of the Year' was printed in large red letters on his sweatshirt. It looked incongruous on his bulging frame. He kept pushing his lank shoulder-length hair away from his face.

Back at the office, Ross found he was overwhelmed by administrative trivia for several hours – performance stats, expenses claims and two reports on recently concluded investigations. It was mid-afternoon before he had time to access the agent log on the system, but there was no trace of Aran Caulfield there. The Brigade also ran a system of Community Monitoring Officers. The 'community' could be a geographical area or a workplace. Basically these people were paid informers. The CMO log was highly protected given its sensitivity. It was early evening before Ross managed to crack the system.

He scrolled through the details. Bingo! Ms A. Caulfield was a lawyer who provided periodic updates on the activities of certain colleagues who defended 'oppositionists' on a regular basis. He would enjoy paying her another visit and this time he might be able to find out a little more about the elusive Carla.

December 14th

Lorna liked the sudden transition from urban overcrowding to the rural isolation of Kintrawe House, but she knew it was early days yet. She sat on the red Turkish rug in front of the fire, next to Laska, listening to the sounds of cooking coming from the kitchen. The rug was covered in small burn marks, the result of sparks spitting at random from the unguarded fire. She wore jeans and a jumper she'd knitted herself that had seen better days.

"So, how are you going to find out anything about your new woman?" she shouted through the open door to the kitchen. Ellis had told her all about his conversation with Ross.

"Apart from going to her address and snooping around a little, I'm not entirely sure. But Ross convinced me that I should make the enquiries. It's just that when I found the body, on my land, in my forest, I felt a responsibility, even though I know that doesn't really make any sense."

Lorna stood up and walked across the room to lean against the frame of the kitchen door. Ellis chopped vegetables for the stew. "Some of these are a bit past it – the frost has got them. I take it you like rabbit?" She nodded. "Good, it's really the only meat I eat, along with a bit of bacon and a few low-flying birds – can't afford any other meat."

He cut the carcass into small pieces, which he coated in flour and then fried in onions, paprika and garlic. The smell woke the dog. The casserole dish was chipped and stained. Ellis filled it with chunks of rabbit, diced vegetables, some stock he'd saved from the previous day and a generous glass of red wine. The dish sat snugly in the middle of the left hand oven. He cut some of his own bread and poured two more glasses of his home-made wine. He and Eric, his neighbour, found it very drinkable, but he'd never tried it out on anyone else. They sat on the sofa watching the logs on the fire settling and sparking. Ellis could see his father out of the corner of his eye, with a wry smile on his face.

"At last! What took you so long? Tora must have been gone a few years now. It's OK – I don't expect an answer, don't want your lady friend to think she's hooked up with a weirdo who talks to himself. I'll leave you to it."

"You still there Ellis? You seemed to disappear for a moment."

"Just drifting off a little in the warmth. Do you fancy a little exercise before we eat – we've got a good hour?"

"What have you got in mind – chopping wood?"

"Not quite." They moved into the bedroom where the temperature dropped about ten degrees, threw off their clothes and slid under the blankets.

"What's this? It's already warm. You must have been planning this, you lecher!"

Ellis moved the hot water bottle to the bottom of the bed and wrapped himself round Lorna.

Late in the evening, as they ate the stew and wiped the rich gravy up with slices of bread, they listened to the jigs and reels on Cairn Radio, one of the small, local stations that sprang up without warning and often disappeared just as quickly.

"So, how would you feel about me helping out with your enquiries?" Lorna's question surprised him. "I mean I'll still have my translation work to do, but I could do some of that here – assuming your broadband's OK." He seemed hesitant. "Look I appreciate you don't really know much about me and that this is sensitive stuff. But as I told you I've got a bit of a track record. The anti-nuke stuff was pretty hairy at times. I'm used to being watched. You can check my credentials online if you want. No – my other credentials," she said in response to his smile.

"I'm just a bit worried," he said. "I think perhaps finding bodies makes me nervous."

Laska suddenly leapt to his feet. His coat bristled and he let out a low growl.

"They're not after us already are they?" Lorna put on a mock worried face.

Ellis went to the window and pulled back the curtain. He could see the wolf standing on the edge of the forest. He went to the kitchen and fished out several pieces of slowly-cooking rabbit from the casserole dish. He threw on his jacket and hat and gestured to Lorna to wait in the house. He slipped out of the front door as she moved to the window.

Was she imagining things? It was a wolf wasn't it? She'd no idea there were wolves anywhere near. She could see Ellis' lips moving as if he was talking to the creature.

He sat in the snow and placed the meat a short distance in front of him. For a while the wolf remained motionless. Lorna wanted to call out, to tell Ellis not to be so foolish. But she kept quiet. The wolf moved slowly towards the meat, ate the scraps and sat again, a few yards away from the man. They watched each other, both seemingly at ease. When the wolf finally moved off into the forest, Ellis continued to sit in the snow, his lips still moving, making gestures with his arms.

Later she asked him about his apparently one-sided conversations. He seemed reluctant to open up at first.

"Obviously my first conversation was with Lucas."

"Who?"

"Lucas – the wolf. He's becoming a good friend. Likes a bite to eat and he's very bright."

"But?" Lorna hesitated. She didn't want to intrude on Ellis' private imaginings. Maybe he was a little odd. All that time he'd spent on his own, with only a few animals around. "Don't you need to remember that it's a wild animal, one with very sharp teeth?"

"He trusts me, I think. Yes of course he could be dangerous, but so's life. After that I was talking to my father – answering him back actually. I never used to dare to do that, but I'm more confident now."

He looked straight at her as if he was talking about a TV programme or a football match. She wasn't sure what to make of this. She thought she remembered him saying his father was dead. She asked him tentatively how the conversation business worked.

"Sorry. I've been doing it so long it's second nature to me. But I've hardly told a soul about it – for obvious reasons. I find our little chats very helpful – clears the mind." She thought there could be something in what he said.

"So what do you think? Am I in or out on your enquiries? I can put my translation work on hold once I've done this piece for the firm in St Petersburg. I can probably get that finished tomorrow. Then I'm all yours, so to speak."

"You're certainly persistent – I'll give you that. Yes, why not, you can help keep me in check."

"That nose of yours is very distinguished you know!"

"What – you mean it's big?"

"No – as I said, distinguished. And I like your hair. Maybe just a wee trim sometime? I bet you used to have a beard. Am I right?"

He nodded. "It made me look like an old man. How about we sort some wood out for the fire, top the wine up and then I can tell you all about what I used to be like."

December 15th

They made an unlikely trio, Toller tall and ungainly, Dommo small and wiry and GPS, nervous-looking with over-sized, thick-framed glasses. There was a shout from somewhere out of sight, over to their right. They climbed up the grassy mound and stood watching two lads, spray cans in hand, working on an elaborate multi-coloured graffiti, totally absorbed in their work.

The trio turned away and continued till they reached the entrance to the old railway tunnel. They liked the tunnels. It was a different world down there. John Tollerson was the bright one. Dominic Muir was no fool, but had to be held back for his own good. GPS was their guide. In fact he was *the* guide. He was a member of a group of tunnel addicts who lived for the buzz of the world below the city. He had an encyclopaedic knowledge of Glasgow's underground geography and an uncanny way of knowing exactly what was located above him, wherever he went.

The tunnel entrance appeared to be completely secure. Toller's head-torch illuminated the steel fencing, cut to fit the arch. There was no obvious sign of a gate. He examined the large sandstone blocks on one side of the arched opening. A drop of cold water splashed down the back of his neck.

"Bastard! Hey, GPS – what's the way in?"

Their guide took a key from his pocket and slid his thin bony wrist through a gap in the fencing. He felt around for the lock on the inside and the key did its job. He pushed inwards on the fencing and a section, hinged on the inside, opened up.

"No bother. Let's go." GPS led the way.

The tunnel, blackened from the days of steam, stretched out ahead of them. They walked at a steady pace, smoking and talking, the tinny rap music from Dommo's phone bouncing off the stone walls. Every few minutes, he would run ahead, torch beam arcing wildly, shout a few obscenities and then return to the others.

"Dommo, you bampot. What you doing on the weed? We need a clear fuckin' head for this, man. It's serious stuff."

"Shut your face, you old man. I'm here to enjoy myself. How much further, GPS, my feet are killing me?"

"Half an hour yet, Dommo. There are quicker routes but this is the easiest way to get in since I had the key cut. What's the plan anyway?"

"The place you told us about, the one with the high security doors. We're going to have a wee shuffty," Toller said grinning. "From what you said about the spec, there must be something in there that's worth a few quid. Our mission is to find out what and maybe get ourselves a sample. As that Colette woman is always telling us – you've got to speculate to accumulate."

"What does she know?" Dommo said dismissively." The other two ignored him.

"So how are you planning to get in?" GPS asked.

"Ah – I've got a little something in here to help us." Toller patted his pocket.

"I'd tuck your trousers into your socks if I were you, lads." GPS bent down and pushed the ends of his combat trousers into his red and white striped socks. "Rats! They're cheeky bastards you know, be up your trousers before you know it."

The other two couldn't tell whether he was taking the piss, but they followed suit. There were occasional narrower, even darker tunnels branching off the main drag. When they heard voices approaching, Dommo looked at Toller and felt for his knife.

"Just some other visitors. Relax man, there's a whole other world down here." GPS walked calmly on, greeted the two men who'd emerged from a small side tunnel and glanced over to Dommo. "What did I say?"

Their torches swayed as they moved forward, casting strange shadows on the arched brick ceiling. There were puddles which covered almost the full width of the tunnel and they had to edge their way along the side wall to escape a soaking.

"More like a bastard assault course," Dommo moaned. "I need a piss." He relieved himself against the wall as the other two walked on. "Don't bloody leave me here for Christ's sake!" He zipped up hurriedly. "Jesus, now I've pissed down my leg." He ran to catch the others up, breathing heavily. He kicked a discarded can against the wall.

The projecting structure loomed out of the darkness sooner than Toller had expected. It was built to fit in with its nineteenth century surroundings and was faced with discarded stone. The steel of the double doors had been tempered to make it look like timber. Oddly they could see no obvious sign of cameras. Toller studied every inch of the structure but could see no point of weakness.

"You're right, GPS. There's some money gone into this. Let's have ourselves a look inside. Where are we by the way? I mean what's above this heap of stone?"

"You're right underneath Central Station."

"Right, spot on. OK, you need to back off now man, you've done your bit."

"Don't worry I'm not hanging around while you two crazies get to work. I'll wait in that recess we passed. If anything goes wrong I'll be off."

"Fair enough."

As GPS receded into the gloom of the tunnel, Toller took a small tin from his pocket and removed a length of plastic explosive. He fixed this to the steel door at a point where he guessed the locking mechanism might be. He embedded the detonator in the plastic and checked the activator. He took two pairs of headphones from his rucksack, put one on and handed the other to his friend.

"This is going to make a wee bit of a noise." The two of them retreated behind a stone buttress. Toller looked at Dommo. "Let's go for it man!"

The explosion sounded more like a naval gun going off. The headphones didn't help much. As the smoke, dust and debris cleared, they could see a gaping hole where the door had been. Dommo whooped and ran off towards the newly created entrance.

"Hold on you lamebrain!" But Dommo couldn't hear a thing. The shooting seemed to come out of nowhere. One minute the figure of Dommo was rushing at full speed towards the shattered opening. The next he was lying in a pool of blood with two armed men standing over him. Toller tried to control his breathing. He felt sick. It wasn't supposed to be like this. Where the fuck had the guards sprung from? He began to edge away from the buttress, feeling his way along the rough stone wall, not daring to use his torch. He tried to remember how far back the recess was. He hoped GPS hadn't left already.

He was in luck, the armed men set off in the opposite direction looking for accomplices. It gave him a little time, but they'd be sure to check his direction as well. It seemed to take an age to reach the recess. GPS was still there. He pointed to his phone. He'd filmed the whole thing. He gestured to Toller to follow.

After a short distance, he led them down a narrow side tunnel, then up a steel ladder. Toller could hardly make his legs work. At the top they found themselves in an abandoned booking hall. The remains of posters hung off the walls advertising day trips to Largs and Rothsay. There was a list of fares in shillings and pence.

GPS pushed on, checking now and then to make sure Toller was following. They walked through a further series of tunnels. Toller was completely lost, his mind a blank. All he could see was Dommo lying in the debris. There was a final ladder and then a large steel hatch which could only be opened from the inside. They emerged into the night onto a canal towpath. Toller collapsed, hyperventilating.

GPS sat beside him studying his phone. He wasn't one for the soothing word, the arm round the shoulder. As far as he was concerned they'd done something extremely stupid and paid the price. But he couldn't just abandon Toller. He'd wait until he was in a fit state to get home. He looked at his phone again. They were definitely Uzis.

December 16th

The not-so-early morning tea in bed was becoming one of their habits. Ellis had no need to be up and out early at this time of the year. He fed Laska, brewed the tea and jumped back under the untidy pile of bedclothes, lying as close as possible to Lorna, to filch some of her warmth.

He was surprised by how quickly he'd taken to having her at Kintrawe and even more surprised that he wasn't obsessing about all the things that might go wrong. Irritations seemed to be at a minimum on both sides. He'd declined to trim his hair despite her suggestion and she'd carried on cleaning up the house, ignoring his comments that most of it was an unnecessary waste of energy. She was able to continue her translation work and had Laska for company when Ellis was out logging.

"When are we going to start our investigations then? I thought we'd have been up and running already."

"You're right – we should get going. It's not exactly cold feet but I'm just a bit wary. How about today if you're up for it?" She nodded. "There's maybe something I should tell you before we get under way so that you're fully in the picture. When I was doing my investigations – sounds good doesn't it – anyway, I met this guy called Lemmy – I don't imagine it's his real name. He told me he'd spoken to Carla, seemed to really like her. He said that he'd mentioned to her about some sort of dirty tricks operation run by the Brigade designed to stir up trouble so that it would be easier for the troublemakers to be rounded up. He was worried that giving her this information might have compromised her. I know we're not going after her now but I felt I ought to tell you, just so you know."

"I think I can cope with that knowledge, but thanks for mentioning it. I've always suspected that the Brig have been involved in that kind of work so it's no surprise really. Maybe it's now more organised than it used to be." Lorna leant across to reach her mug of tea from the bedside table and took a few sips. He could see the outline of her body through her nightdress. He was very easily distracted.

"Oh, by the way, did you see that special delivery parcel? I left it on the table for you last night."

"No, I didn't. I was half asleep by the time I got back from Eric's." He and Eric spent evenings together when they swapped stories and tried to drink each other under the table.

"And full of whisky judging by your breath. I'll get it for you."

The special delivery envelope was addressed to Ellis Landsman in large, black, felt tip capitals. He tore the bag open. Inside was a phone and a typed note which stated – "*Incoming only, my way of keeping you up to date.*"

"Who's that from – your friend Ross?"

"It must be. He said he'd set up some way for us to keep in touch, without using what he called normal channels."

+ + +

Ellis came in from loading fence posts on to a customer's trailer. The wind was raw and his face was chapped. He took off his boots and sat in front of the fire which Lorna had set and lit. Laska was in his usual winter position on the hearthrug.

"So – what's our starting point? Where did Rebecca Leuchars live?" Lorna was keen to get started.

"Oh, it's somewhere up in Maryhill, a place called Retiro Gardens House. Odd name. Ross said it was near the Partick Thistle ground."

"I know where that is."

"Right, shall we go then?"

"At last! I thought we'd never get going. I could do with picking up a change of clothes from the flat. Bring the dog and we can stay at mine tonight if you like. It'll give us more time." Lorna stared into the flames. "Bit of a waste of a good fire though. I've only just got it going. Oh, and the translation's finished and sent."

Travelling with someone else improved Ellis' spirits. The sun was bright, the trees swayed in a strong, cold easterly, the train was almost on time. He'd had a delivery of diesel the previous day so they could have taken the Land Rover, but he thought he should go sparingly with the fuel. Besides he was getting to like the train rides.

"What do you fancy doing for Christmas then? My place or yours?" He had decided to abandon his usual Hebridean Christmas. Lorna smiled, delighted that he had asked her.

"Oh, I think Kintrawe would be better, all those Christmas trees surrounding the house, plenty of snow, very seasonal. Are we allowed to eat one of the chickens?"

"That's so heartless. My little friends. But yes, I suppose we could."

From Queen Street station they caught a bus up to Maryhill and then asked in a betting shop near the football ground, if they knew where Retiro Gardens House was. The man behind the counter barely took his eyes away from the TV screen as he answered.

"What's left of it is up by the canal, just next to Wilkinson's garage. Used to be a lovely spot till the squatters moved in. Mind, it had been empty for months, so the owners were asking for it really. From what I've heard, the ground floor and the stairs are none too happy, so watch your step if you're going in."

The canal basin was deserted. A large, three-storey, double fronted house that had clearly seen better days stood in an overgrown garden. A number of cars in varying stages of decay were parked haphazardly on the drive. They walked up to the front door and knocked. As this generated no response, they tried hammering instead.

"OK, OK, where's the fuckin' fire?" A man in a dressing gown pulled back the door and squinted at them. "What do youse want?"

Ellis explained they were friends of Rebecca's. "She's not been here for a while. Wait here, I'll get her feller." They waited.

Eventually a haggard looking man emerged. He hadn't bothered with a dressing gown, just a pair of red striped pyjamas which looked incongruous on the doorstep. "Yes?"

Ellis explained for the second time. "Did you know Rebecca?"

The man looked at first as if he didn't understand the question, but then it became clear that he was trying to control his emotions. "Is she dead then?"

Ellis was taken aback by the bluntness of the response. "Look, I'm really sorry, but yes I'm afraid she is. I found her. She was buried on my land. I promised myself I'd try and find out what happened to her."

"How did you get her address?"

"I asked the Brig and they told me eventually. That's why it's taken some time."

"So, when did you find her?"

"It must be a couple of weeks ago now. Look I'm really sorry but I thought you should know and I couldn't rely on the Brig telling you. I don't imagine they'll be doing much investigating either. Can we come in?"

The man led them into a large, sparsely furnished front room. The floor creaked and one or two boards were missing. He opened the curtains cautiously as if he was worried about the effects of too much daylight. Ellis noticed a variety of drug-related paraphernalia scattered around the room. They sat in the window seat and listened while the man told them about Bex, as he called her. He was clearly shattered by the news, kept stopping to pace up and down the room, twisting and untwisting a handkerchief around his wrist. Ellis felt he shouldn't push him too much but he wanted to find out more.

"Any chance of a cup of tea?" he asked.

"Aye – sorry, not really thinking. Tom, by the way – Tom Cavanagh. That's a nice dog you've got." He walked slowly off to the kitchen and returned a few minutes later with three mugs of very strong tea.

"Could you maybe tell us how you knew Bex and anything that might have happened recently you think might be important?"

It took a while for Cavanagh to wind himself up. His voice was shaky to start with but he grew more confident as he went on.

"I don't want to believe it. I mean I know she was up to her ears in problems but to disappear like that and then to die. It's a terrible thing to happen." He paused and took a deep breath. "I first met her at the Dive. It's closed since, but it was underneath one of the railway arches, right in the middle of town. It was their Trance night. She looked out of it but I think it was just the music. We just started talking, about the sounds and then about anything really. Turned out I knew her brother, but not well. He's a waster. She said it before I did, so it was cool.

"We left about four, picked up the usual disgusting kebab and got the night bus back here. I hadn't intended to sleep with her. No, really, but somehow it just happened. My room is at the top of the house, so we can get a bit of peace and quiet. The headcases on the bottom floor were out, as luck would have it. I've had far fewer women than people think – must be something about my manner. But she was good."

Ellis looked at the floor and felt uncomfortable, felt he was intruding, which of course he was. Lorna seemed to take it in her stride. Cavanagh coughed, spat into his hankie and continued.

"We were together 24/7 at first. It sort of felt a bit intense but we were both hooked. And she didn't take anything for the first few days. But once she started, she changed, became all withdrawn, scared at times too, as if someone was after her. Of course, someone was after her. He turned up when we were in this bar. She hadn't let on she was a regular, but everyone seemed to be catching her eye. He just walked right up to her, ignoring me completely, demanding payment. He was a weasel-looking guy, trousers tucked into socks, cheap trainers, football top – some strip I didn't recognise but then I don't know much about footy. He was holding his phone, glancing at it, then at her. When he moved right up to her and started jabbing his finger I told him to leave it. He completely ignored me. My upper body's quite short so people get the wrong impression when I'm sitting down. He backed off as soon as I stood up but kept on with his ranting. I told him to shut it. He kicked the table over, drinks all over the place and stormed off. I had to calm the barman down. He was all for throwing us out. Bex was in a bad way. On the walk home, between her coughing and spluttering, she spilled out the sorry story of her dealing. The Weasel was just the messenger. A guy called Trawden was the one she was stressing over."

"Do you know who this Trawden guy is, where he lives?" Lorna asked, keen to move things on. She could see he didn't want to answer. "It's just that we could follow things up if we knew."

"He's not a man to mess with. I can't say more than that." Cavanagh's hands were shaking and he spilled some of his tea over his pyjamas.

"That's OK," said Lorna. "Hopefully we can track him down. How was Bex when you last saw her?"

"Not so good really. We never managed to get that laid-back feeling again. Everything went downhill. We argued all the time, the sex stopped, she was out of it for longer and longer.

"The day Trawden came to the house was the worst. He looked insignificant apart from his eyes which were completely cold. He talked about people who'd come to a nasty end and I'd no reason to think he was making it up. He wanted the two grand that he said Bex owed. She had about £500 and I'd nothing. Trawden took her money and told her he wanted the rest within a day. He reminded her about what had happened to his other debtors.

"Bex seemed to give in at that point. I made various half-baked suggestions about how we might be able to raise the money but she wasn't really interested, just sat there rocking backwards and forwards, chain smoking. I told her we could leave, fly off somewhere – not that we had any money. She looked straight at me, completely beaten. She'd told me a bit about her past. This wasn't the first time she'd been threatened over debts. Trawden had told her about others who'd just disappeared. *I've got a nice little plot lined up for you* was his favourite phrase apparently. People disappear all the time of course, a wee snippet in the paper and the Brig going through the motions. No-one's interested in feuds between low life.

"That's about it really. One day she just didn't turn up. We were supposed to meet in this café just off Trongate but she didn't show. I never saw her again." Cavanagh looked exhausted. They knew they wouldn't get any more out of him.

"Thanks for all this. I know it must have been really hard for you. Look if you think of anything else, give me a ring." Ellis handed him a card with his phone number on. As he and Lorna left the room, Cavanagh curled up in a ball on the sofa.

* December 17th

Christ it was a shock. As I was walking home last night – well my temporary home anyway – this man came alongside me. I couldn't see him very well in the half-light. He told me he was a senior officer from the Brigade, seemed to know about the new me, mentioned C's name. There was something about him, not exactly creepy, but not a man to trust. I've been half expecting something like this to happen but it's still a shock. It was obvious he knew about my job – my new job, but he wasn't at all specific. Then he asked me to come for a drink. He wasn't threatening, but I felt I couldn't refuse. I needed to find out more about him and work out how to handle him.

He had it all worked out, and we went this hotel lounge bar just round the corner. It had those very plush seats that are hard to get out of, long expensive looking curtains, waiters who hover only when you need them. Not my sort of place at all. He insisted on cocktails.

In the light of the bar I suddenly recognised him, tall, imposing, shaved head, the top man himself, Commander Daid. All the bosses keep a low profile – for security reasons they claim. But I'd seen his picture somewhere. Never actually met him before – not at my level. I tried to keep my nerve, keep steady.

He told me he was pleased with what I'd done so far and that he had some additional work in mind, information he wanted me to provide directly to him. We were sitting side by side and his hand strayed slowly to my leg. I edged away without trying to be too obvious. He didn't seem to be the slightest bit embarrassed, just tried the manoeuvre again.

I left for the toilet and on my return sat rather pointedly at the far end of the sofa. He continued with his smooth talking, told me I'd need to meet him the following day to get details of the information he wants me to provide directly to him. He reminded me it was nearly Christmas, which I'd completely forgotten about, and gave me the name of this swanky hotel where we'd be meeting.

When I said I'd have to check it out with C, he told me that wouldn't be necessary. In fact I'd be jeopardising my position if I did. This started to really worry me. As he left, he told me to take care and said it was a shame I couldn't spend Christmas with Ms Caulfield, as he called her. That really set the alarm bells ringing. I don't know what to make of it all. The only thing that's clear is that I can't trust him an inch – and that I can't ignore him.

The volume of stuff that's coming off the feeds is overwhelming. We seem to be trawling every organisation bar the Mother's Union – and maybe they're next. But we're picking up some serious information as well, not as bad as Meikle and his gang, but quite hardcore. Some of the suspects seem to disappear. Whether they do literally, I don't know. And the girls were talking about one of the agents who'd terminated a suspect. The agents send their reports to us on their X20's, so we get to know most of what's going on out in the field. Not everything though. A few of their reports go straight to Morrisey.

We use all the info we get to classify suspect organisations into various categories – arrest and detain immediately, arrest and bail, shut-downs, harassments, and shake downs (where the organisation has a bit of money)!

It's all under the TTT mantra of course, which these days covers just about anything. There's a TV advert they've been running for a while, which features clips from various demonstrations, with the theme that it's a slippery slope from demonstrating to terrorism. The ad ends with the 'Tackling Terrorism Together' banner blowing in *the wind and an authoritative voiceover using the all too familiar phrase – 'you can't be too careful.'*

The job of the agents in the field is to plant evidence, doctor websites, encourage the hotheads, all undercover of course. We send them encrypted details of new targets, particularly unions – what's left of them, environmental groups, any kind of direct action outfit, the wrong kind of lobbyists. Some of them object, threaten legal action, but they don't get anywhere. I'm giving C his summarised version of all this. I think there's more going on, more serious stuff but so far I've only picked up hints. C says this is what he's really after and that when he gets the right kind of dirt, it can be used to pull the plug on the operation. I think I believe him.

With the Daid thing happening, I almost forgot about the chaos at work, a couple of days ago. They wouldn't tell us what had gone on, but we got the story from the guards. There are always two of them on duty. Apparently a nutcase tried to break in through the emergency exit, using some sort of explosive. Just a kid, they said. Of course by the time the story got higher up the organisation it had morphed into a full scale terrorist attack. We didn't even know there was an emergency exit. It's obviously not there for our benefit. The damage was superficial and it hasn't interrupted our work at all. Embarrassing for the boss though – apparently the cameras down there weren't working.

December 18th

Commander Daid scanned the room at the waterside reception. It was the venue for one of the bigger junkets, the annual security awards, full of pointless backslapping and bonhomie. He spotted one of the senior executives from Great Wall, a tall attractive woman he knew from his Hong Kong days. He began to edge across the room towards her, greeting people as he passed, people he didn't want to talk to.

His mind wouldn't focus properly. He didn't like the way things were developing. He'd never considered himself to be a cautious man. God knows he'd taken enough risks in the past. But it got harder. It definitely got harder. He never used to feel the pressure but now it was getting to him. The neck massages helped of course. He thought about his masseuse – what was her name – Macy? That was something Tanny couldn't do. He did miss Pelham's wife, hadn't seen her for days, but there were always other opportunities.

He spotted Pelham at the far end of the room and took care to avoid eye contact. He couldn't seem to escape the bloody man. His confrontational manner at the racecourse had startled Daid. He'd never seen him like that before. But of course it had become personal. Apart from the business with Tanny, Pelham had since made it plain that he knew all about Daid's other extra-curricular activities. He wondered where Pelham got his information from. He wasn't aware of being followed, hacked or bugged. Then there was the business of the joint working with Great Wall. Pelham had stuck a spanner in the works here as well. And to make things worse, Pelham had the ear of Brigadier Michael Cutting at the Pyramid and was feeding him a steady anti-Daid diet.

He could see that if he wasn't careful, he'd be marginalised and his star would begin to wane. At least he'd be able to get some useful ammunition from Lucini. She was a cold fish but he was confident his charms would have their effect sooner rather than later.

He had to admit the whisky was very good, one of the rarer malts. He finally emerged from the scrum of guests and found himself standing next to the woman from Great Wall. He greeted her and kissed her on both cheeks. They talked about Hong Kong and the changes. He suggested meeting up for a meal and she was clearly interested, in that and maybe more. He kept a discreet eye on Pelham as he over-indulged in his usual style.

The boat commissioned to take guests home pulled up at the riverside venue. Daid noticed Pelham slumping into one of the plush seats at the front of the boat, and then made his way to his favourite position, at the back of the catamaran, his head hanging over the side, breathing in the heady mix of diesel fumes and river effluent. The engine roared. The lights reflected in the dull metal water.

He was on his own. For a moment he was able to clear his mind and just stare at the swirling water. But the moment passed and his doubts resurfaced. What should he do? How soon would word about his indiscretions get out? What would Pelham do to try and bring him down? Glasgow could be so bloody small and word circulated so quickly.

The door from the warm interior of the boat opened and an all too familiar figure walked unsteadily out onto the open deck.

"Daid! Thought I might find you here. Need some fresh air?"

It was all Daid could do to stop himself from telling his superior to fuck off.

"You're building up quite a rap sheet as the Yanks would say. First it's you screwing around with Tanny and God knows how many other women, then it's you fouling up your performance and losing out to the Chinese and now I hear your man Cormack is sticking his big nose into things that are nothing to do with him."

Daid was immediately on his guard. What had the bastard heard now? He'd have to tread very carefully.

"Cormack and I did you a favour, Pelham. If you hadn't taken your eye off the ball we'd have had no need to get involved in Darkstone."

"Don't you dare talk to me like that!"

The spray was increasing as the boat moved through a particularly choppy section of water. They were finding it harder and harder to hear each other.

"Those two agents you recommended to me. From what I've heard they're supplying Cormack with certain incriminating operational details, with the aim of discrediting Darkstone and getting one over the Pyramid. It doesn't take a genius to work out what you're up to." Pelham was slurring his words. "You want to dish the dirt and then come in as Mr Clean and take over the running of the unit. God knows what would happen then. Well I can tell you now it ain't going to happen. I've put up with a lot from you and told nobody about it. I can't do that any longer. When I've had my say, you'll be finished."

Daid noticed that Pelham was looking increasingly pale, probably the combined effects of the drink and the movement of the boat across the choppy water.

He stared across to the riverbank. He was close to getting somewhere with Darkstone. Could he believe Pelham – that he'd not shared his suspicions with anyone else yet? How could he have worked it out? There hadn't been any leaks as far as he was aware – unless someone was playing for both sides. He was confident about Cormack, wasn't he? But what about the woman? Was she feeding Pelham? Or was it just in Pelham's head. He was a clever bastard after all.

Yes, he reckoned that was it – Pelham having a moment of inspiration. *You can never trust someone like Daid. He'll always be looking after number one. He'll never be able to leave something like Darkstone alone, until he controls it. I'll confront him – study his reaction.*

"You're way off beam, Pelham, as usual. I did you a good turn, found you two excellent agents within your ludicrous timescale and now you throw it back in my face. As for the contract, our performance has been good and you know it. For some reason you've developed this vendetta against me. It can't all be down to Tanny. You two haven't got on for years."

"How dare you say anything about my wife and me!" Pelham spoke in a hoarse, exaggerated whisper. Daid could smell his fetid breath. "What can you possibly know about our life together? And don't think for an instant that I blame her for this. You're notorious for not being able to keep your pants on. You're completely compromised. You're shameless and the sooner London knows about this the better."

Daid was caught off-guard by this sudden vehemence and the look of hatred. He glanced towards the two sets of closed doors that led into the saloon area. He couldn't see any passengers in the rear seats. The open deck was in shadow, the sky dark and cloudy, the wind freshening. He needed to make a decision, an immediate decision, before they reached the pier. Pelham was leaning over the rail staring at a huge crane on the construction site on the near bank. The jib was covered in a thin trail of fairylights and there was a token Christmas tree stuck on the end. The new structure was half completed, rising up from a sea of builders' cabins that littered the site. A large sign announced *Christmas Greetings from HKJ Construction.*

Daid moved rapidly. It only took light pressure at the base of Pelham's neck and a sharp movement to adjust the body position. The splash was barely audible. It wasn't the first time he'd killed a man but it was the first time he'd taken a grim pleasure in it. He counted to twenty and then shouted. He ran through the heat of the saloon, startling passengers and sprinted up the stairs to the bridge.

"Jesus – man overboard, man overboard!"

The captain stared at him as his co-pilot immediately pulled back the throttle. The craft juddered violently. The turn was slow and cumbersome. As they began to retrace the route, a spotlight hovered over the surface of the river. Daid told them where he thought the man should be. He made sure they were slightly downstream from the true position. Eventually he suggested they move upstream a touch. They saw the body up against the wharf side. They launched the small rubber dinghy with difficulty and towed the body to the bottom of the steps that led down from the embankment.

+ + +

When he was interviewed in the early hours of the morning, Daid explained that Pelham had been unsteady on his feet because of the amount of drink he'd consumed. He had stumbled heavily against the boat's low rail and toppled over into the river. It had taken a while for the catamaran to come to a halt and then turn and by the time the body had been located, it had been too late. It had been difficult for Daid to remember exactly where the fall had taken place. He stressed how emotional it had been, losing such a close colleague.

He eventually reached home about four in the morning. He was confident that he wouldn't be under any suspicion. He'd taken care over the years to hide his antipathy to Pelham and the man was well known for his inability to hold his drink.

But Daid couldn't be certain that Pelham hadn't already shared his suspicions and concerns with the Pyramid. For the first time in his career, he felt vulnerable.

December 19th

Lorna tidied away the breakfast things and fetched her coat. Ellis re-read the text on the new phone. They'd been dithering about trying to track down Trawden, unsure of what risks they might be taking. *You may want to talk to William Trawden. He lives in Milngavie. Ask around for his address, he's well known. Watch your step with him.*

Ellis was puzzled. How did Ross know they were after Trawden. Maybe it was some link he'd dug up between Trawden and Rebecca in his research. Ellis tried to phone Ross but got only his voicemail.

They went by bus to Milngavie, sitting on the front seats on the top deck, with Laska snoozing on the floor. They'd picked up a couple of samosas at the Asian supermarket, fresh and hot, the flaky pastry dropping on the bus floor, from where it was hoovered up by the dog. A couple of kids sitting opposite tried poking him with their shoes but Lorna's look was enough to make them stop.

When they got off the bus, they went into the nearest shop and asked where Trawden lived. The woman told them that the Trawden residence was at the top end of Deal Street and gave them directions. They decided to walk. As they went through the park a group of affluent young mothers moved slowly past, their buggies as well equipped as small cars.

'Heights of Deal' did in fact stand on a small hill. Ellis thought the name suggested that at least the man had a sense of humour.

The electronic gates were firmly closed. The voice on the intercom informed them that Mr Trawden was not at home. They perched on the garden wall and leaned up against the ornate wrought iron railings trying to decide what to do. They were in luck. A large Jaguar swept up the road and stopped to await the opening of the gates. Lorna took her opportunity and waved at the driver. He lowered his window just enough for a conversation.

"Would Mr Trawden be so kind as to grant us five minutes? We just need a little information about Rebecca Leuchars." The driver turned to speak to his rear seat passenger. The rear window was lowered.

"You have your five minutes and no longer." Trawden spoke almost without moving his lips.

Ellis explained why they were there, without mentioning Tom Cavanagh, identifying the Brigade as the source of his information. He said he just wanted a name to help him further his enquiries, and wondered whether Mr Trawden might be able to provide this. Trawden stepped out of the car, stretched and waved his driver on through the open gates. He bent down to tickle the dog under his neck.

"The man you want is a Mr McPhee. Lives up in the Outlands I believe, close to Loch Airne. I wish you both a safe journey home." With that he walked through the slowly closing gates and disappeared up the drive.

"That name rings a bell," Ellis said, staring at the slowly closing gates.

"Someone you know?" Lorna asked, surprised.

"Dunno. I've just come across the name recently, but can't think where. How about a bite to eat and then back to yours?"

"Sounds good to me. I didn't like the look of him, did you?" Ellis shook his head.

It was dark by the time they reached Partick station and they walked slowly to the flat. As Lorna kicked off her shoes and put the kettle on, Laska settled down in front of the gas fire. Ellis said he'd nip upstairs to see if Gam and Colette were in. He hadn't seen them for nearly a fortnight and wanted to exchange notes. When he knocked, Colette answered the door and he could tell straight away that something was seriously wrong. She beckoned him in to the living room. Gam was talking to a lad who was holding his head in his hands.

"You couldn't have known, Toller. I mean using the explosives was not necessarily the wisest move, but from what you've said that was Dommo's bright idea anyway. But – armed guards in a disused tunnel, nobody could have expected that."

Ellis was confused. Colette ushered him into the kitchen and brought him up to speed. Toller was one of her students. He'd been there when Dommo, a friend of his, had been shot and killed by security guards. She told him about the ill-fated expedition in the disused tunnel, about how the lads had hoped that something valuable would be behind the security doors. Toller and his underground guide had managed to escape. He'd been lying low for a few days and had then made it to Colette's flat.

"He's going to have to disappear for a while," she told Ellis. "It's likely he'll have been picked up on camera with Dommo, prior to the explosion and the shooting, in which case the Brig will be after him. He's in a right state, all his usual belligerence has vanished. Gam doesn't want him here in the flat and I agree with him. He's far too much of a risk and if he was caught here, it would give the Brig the perfect excuse to put Gam away for a long stretch. And I'd be out of a job."

"He could come with me," Ellis said, immediately wondering why he'd made such a stupid suggestion. "I mean it's a possibility, I've no connection with him, we're in the middle of nowhere, he could even do some work for me if he was up for it. Oh and by the way, you know Lorna your neighbour, well we're sort of together now." He looked and felt a bit embarrassed.

Colette's worried face softened momentarily. "We should obviously have kept a closer eye on you two. You sly dogs! Wait here a mo and I'll speak to Gam, and put your suggestion to Toller – as long as you're sure. It's still a risk you know. After all, the Brig will class what they did as an act of terrorism."

This was Ellis' chance to back out. He stayed silent and Colette went into the living room.

Colette took a while, but eventually she managed to persuade Toller that he should go with Ellis. He hadn't really taken much notice of Ellis as he'd moved through the living room, but he'd immediately classed him as a bit of a weirdo, longish hair, old clothes, posh sounding voice. But he knew staying in the city was too dangerous.

Toller sat in a separate carriage from Ellis and Lorna on the train journey. They thought they'd stick out like a sore thumb as a trio. He left the station at Alexandria on his own and walked the first quarter of a mile until he was out of range of any cameras before they picked him up in the Land Rover. He said barely a word on the journey to Ellis' place, but seemed to take to Laska quickly enough.

Ellis arranged for him to sleep in the old bunk house, which had been well used in years gone by but had been closed up for a while. Ellis instructed him about the stove, which he seemed to grasp quickly enough. He asked if Laska could stay with him and Ellis said if it was OK with the dog it was OK with him.

When Ellis told Lorna the full story, she was worried. Anyone who dealt with explosives might be involved in all sorts of other illegal activity. With the Brig on the look-out, they'd have to be careful. But she knew it was Ellis' decision and she could always leave if she didn't like it. She decided to stay and go along with it, at least for the time being.

Ellis sat up late after the excitement of the day. It was strange without the dog and there was no sign of the wolf. His father took the opportunity to make an appearance. He was sat in his usual seat, at one side of the fire, stroking his chin in his old familiar way.

"You like to keep things simple don't you?"

"Look if you're going to start I'm going to bed."

"No, no, just making a comment. I mean the boy's obviously a little immature, to put it mildly."

"Look if he'd stayed where he was, he'd have been picked up – absolutely certain. He's from a Class Three Estate. I thought I could help in a small way. And at the end of the day the only person who suffered from their stupidity was his mate."

"So, what about when the Brig come snooping round here?"

"I don't think they will. They did the break-in and found nothing. I'm no longer looking for Carla. And the real body is of no interest to them as far as I'm aware."

"You and Lorna seem to be getting on well."

"Yes, we do, don't we? I didn't see it coming at all. Is there anything you don't keep track of?"

December 20ᵗʰ

Daid had heard from his contact at the Pyramid. Apparently they'd taken Pelham's death in their stride. He'd been due to retire within twelve months anyway and his sudden departure would give them the opportunity to get a younger, more dynamic man installed as his replacement. It was time to sharpen things up.

Daid had even been the recipient of some sympathy – having had to witness the drowning of a close colleague and the macabre search for the body. Although London had made an immediate interim appointment as head of SecureScotland, Daid felt he would be in a good position to exploit the temporary power vacuum.

This was all on the plus side. On the downside, he was concerned about Cormack's recent behaviour. The man was so damned efficient, but, worryingly, he also seemed to be very effective at accumulating power. Daid had to admit that the Major was doing an excellent job on Darkstone. The information he was feeding through was first rate. But Daid suspected Cormack would be filtering if not censoring the information, in order to consolidate his own power base. That was why he'd decided to set up his own direct supply line. He glanced at the photo of the 'new' Carla Lucini. She was definitely his type. He looked forward to their next liaison at the Biarritz.

With Pelham out of the way, he was getting the negotiations with Chen's team at Great Wall back on track. He knew Chen from their Hong Kong days. Oddly the dirt they had on each other provided a degree of trust. They'd even talked about a strategy for getting rid of SecureScotland altogether. As kings of the Scottish Central Belt they'd be a powerful outfit. Their plans could save millions and provide a more effective service. Daid knew this was just the sort of proposal the Pyramid would want to hear about.

He and Chen would speak to Brigadier Cutting in London when the time was right. But Daid knew they'd have to play their cards carefully, otherwise Cutting would see him just like he viewed Cormack – as an empire builder.

+ + +

As he climbed the stairs again to Aran Caulfield's flat, Ross Lambert congratulated himself that at least he'd got over the first hurdle. She'd let him in. That same cold stare greeted him as she opened the front door to the apartment and nodded for him to come in. He'd just mentioned her law firm when he'd spoken to her on the entry phone and that had been sufficient for the door to open. The apartment was as warm and tidy as it had been on his previous visit. Nothing seemed to be out of place. With two young boys at home, Ross' home was in constant turmoil.

"Thank you for agreeing to speak to me. I'm sorry our previous discussion didn't go too well. That was my fault. Look I know about Carla, well enough to know that she's still alive and kicking. She's your lodger, but she's not registered to live here. As I said before that's a concern to me. But maybe it's got something to do with your position as a Community Monitoring Officer." He left the comment hanging.

Aran couldn't work out how to respond to this man. She'd been told by the Brigade that nobody else knew about Carla and her new life. How had this man found out and was he a danger? What were his real motives?

"Well Sergeant, all I can say is that the Brigade approved Carla's residence here even though it isn't her registered address. As you've deduced she's not living here now and I don't know where she is. I'm not at liberty to say what's happened and in fact it could be dangerous for her if any information leaked out. As a Brigade officer yourself, I'm sure you'll appreciate that."

So she was still alive. His guess had been right. That was enough for the time being. Ross felt if he pushed any further, it might get dangerous.

+ + +

Aran Caulfield closed the front door behind the Sergeant and made a call on her mobile.

"Yes, it's fine. The coast is clear now."

Ten minutes later she heard a key in the door. Iain Cormack entered the room, placed the carefully wrapped presents on the dining table and kissed her on the cheek.

"Ah, that's so nice of you, Iain. Yours are in the carrier over there. Can't believe it's almost Christmas. Where has the time gone? Are you sure it's OK visiting again so soon?" she asked as she disappeared from the room.

She brought drinks from the kitchen and curled up on the sofa.

"No, it's not a problem, sis." Cormack sat in the leather armchair, which comfortably accommodated his stocky frame. Once he was in the chair he was always reluctant to leave it. He sipped the cranberry juice. He'd given up alcohol years ago – had seen too much of its downside on too many colleagues.

"You know Pelham – well of him anyway? Well he's dead." Aran looked shocked. Cormack told her what had happened.

"Does his death have any implications for you?" she asked. Cormack smiled.

"Nothing negative. Could even be some opportunities. He was such a dinosaur – just like Daid really."

"God I nearly forgot. Carla told me that the Commander has been creeping around her and asking for information. He told her to provide him with information directly even though he's getting briefed by you."

"Very interesting. Thanks for that Aran. When you say creeping around, do you mean sexually?"

"Exactly! Poor girl sounded really upset."

"Well, I'll have to see what I can do about Mr Daid and his activities. But what news of our friend Lambert?"

"Oh yes, he's more than a little off piste. He obviously has no difficulty hacking into Brigade records, certainly has all my details, knows about my CMO status. And he's worked out, somehow, that Carla is still alive. I'm worried – could this be dangerous for her?"

"I don't think so. I've checked him out myself. He seems pretty straight but he's a friend of a man called Ellis Landsman. They went to college together. Landsman was the one who found the body – the one that wasn't Carla. He was getting too interested in her, so I ordered Lambert to divert him and get him to concentrate his efforts on the real owner of the body so to speak. It was a woman called Rebecca Leuchars. I've got my own reasons for wanting information on her and it's much better for the digging to be done by someone outside the Brigade. But enough of him. What about you? How are you coping without Carla?"

"I don't like it one little bit, but I know it's necessary – for her safety. Will it really be two months?"

"I think so."

"She'll be very worried about her parents. What exactly were they told?"

Very rarely for him, Cormack looked almost embarrassed. He coughed.

"It was all a little awkward, sis. Landsman beat us to it. By the time my man paid the parents a courtesy call, they'd already been told she was dead. So we had no choice but to go along with that. Of course they weren't asked to ID the body and we persuaded the mother to have a small ceremony in the Brigade Chapel rather than anything public. It wasn't ideal but we did what was necessary."

Aran looked at her brother open-mouthed.

"So, how's all that going to be unravelled when the time comes?"

"Oh we'll set Landsman up to take the fall for it. Anyway to be brutally honest, I'm not sure the old woman will last that long and the father hasn't a clue what's going on anyway. You've never met them have you?"

"No, Carla wanted to keep us as far apart as possible. But it'll hit her hard when she finds out. You really don't have any morals, do you, Iain?"

* December 21ˢᵗ

I really don't know what to do about Mr Daid. I told Aran about him on the phone and said I was going to tell C. But she advised me against this, said to wait and see how things developed. I've sent Val some extra detail for the log he's keeping, so at least there's a record if it all goes wrong.

I didn't finish work until eight today. The sooner Christmas is over with, the better as far as I'm concerned. But I'm looking forward to the coach trip and lunch on the 25ᵗʰ. At least it will get me out of Glasgow.

After work I went as instructed by Daid to the Hotel Biarritz. It's one of those swanky upmarket places full of false everything, a supposedly Michelin starred restaurant and the Skyline Bar on the 23ʳᵈ floor which is where we met. I have to say there's a great view from the bar. You can see the M8 snaking through city and beyond to the Clyde. Well, as it was dark, all I could see was the lights, but they're impressive enough. And then further out, just darkness with the occasional pinpoint of light. When Daid arrived, he wanted to know all about C and what he'd instructed me to do. I said I wasn't authorised to tell anyone anything. He started telling me about C and about my role, sort of proving that I could be open with him.

I was cautious to start with, but then there didn't seem too much point in holding back. He seemed particularly interested in some of things I mentioned and made notes in a little black book. I wonder what else is in there. He tried the touching business again, with the same response from me. No effect – he just kept coming back. Eventually something in me snapped. I told him that if he knew all about me which he obviously did, then he'd know I lived with a woman and wasn't interested in men. He kept quite calm and said that didn't mean he wasn't interested in me. But at least he backed off a little.

He went into business mode and told me in detail the kind of information he wants me to send him to send him each day. So that's two logs I have to do now, on top of the stuff I pull together for my legal man. It's a pity I can't just send one email copied to the three of them. That would put the cat amongst the pigeons!

At the end of our little discussion he told me he'd booked a room for us. He didn't blink, just waited for me to stand up and start walking with him to the lift. I'm afraid I lost it and told him that if he mentioned it again, or tried touching me again, I'd scream the place down. You could see him weighing it up, whether it would be worth it. Eventually he smiled that awful, creepy smile of his and said he liked a girl with spirit.

As I waited for the express lift to the ground floor, I could see him eyeing up another girl. He probably didn't want to waste the room booking.

December 22nd

Michael Cutting pushed a strand of his still blond hair away from his eyes and settled his long legs into the large leather chair. He'd seen most things before. He'd learnt when to intervene and when to just let nature take its course. His empire continued to expand. Underneath the security umbrella, all sorts of strange bedfellows slept comfortably together. It was the only area of Government expenditure not subject to constant cut backs. On the contrary, it was a positive growth area. This made it easy in some ways. But it also meant that it could become a breeding ground for almost any kind of crackpot idea that could be badged in some way as important for the country's security.

He was adept at spotting winners and losers. Darkstone had actually been one of his ideas, to allow, indeed, encourage the opposition to dig its own grave. To him, it didn't really matter how 'the opposition' was defined. His view was that, in a democracy, as long as you allowed for periodic elections and had at least some semblance of a free press, opposition wasn't necessary, except perhaps as a safety valve. He preferred to be the one who decided how that valve should be calibrated.

Pelham's death had been an inconvenience but not much more than that. He didn't for a minute believe that it had been an accident, even allowing for Pelham's close association with alcohol. But he saw no point in trying to pin the death on Daid. It would be almost impossible to prove and would create an almighty mess.

Besides he had other plans involving Daid. Pelham's death had given him the opportunity he'd been waiting for to reshape services in Scotland and if the changes worked, then England would be next.

Cutting adjusted his silk tie and glanced at Iain Cormack who looked completely at home, comfortably seated at the other side of the large mahogany desk. He'd kept a close eye on Cormack's progress ever since the early days when he'd spent part of his career at the Pyramid. Cutting reflected that it was a good job that Charles Daid had never been made aware of Cormack's early links with the centre of power. And then there'd been his success in breaking the opposition to the continuation of Trident in Scotland. Cormack had become hot property after that and Daid had managed to capture him.

"So, Iain, how long before you're after my job?" The flash of teeth couldn't really be described as a smile. Cormack looked almost embarrassed.

"Well, I don't know about that, sir. But I do have a little information for you. As you know I've set up the Darkstone conduit and it's producing nicely. As we suspected, Mr Morrisey doesn't appear to know the limits of legality and Mr Pelham's oversight was perhaps somewhat lacking in this respect. With regard to Mr Daid, I've been able to gather most of the necessary evidence and the final pieces of the jigsaw should be put into place within the next week or so.

"As far as the new contract goes, you'll no doubt be aware that he and Mr Chen have been in close co-operation. They plan to cover the Central Belt between them. I'm pretty sure the Commander would then use this position of strength to propose a takeover of SecureScotland. He'd justify this by the significant cost savings such a change would generate – you know, scrapping the old divisions, getting rid of duplicated bureaucracies."

Cutting nodded. He reflected on how closely these plans matched his own. What was there not to like about less bureaucracy, more efficiency and significantly lower costs? Cutting chuckled to himself as he thought about the one difference between Daid's plan and his own. His plan for the new future had no place for the current Commander. He realised that Cormack was still ploughing on, telling him something about the technical and legal background to the proposed changes. He'd heard enough.

"That's very interesting, Iain. As usual you're bang up to date, finger on the pulse. Are you confident you can keep Landsman under control? From what I hear he's very much the maverick. I'm always a little worried about loose cannons."

"He needs watching, but he can do what we can't. He's a little slow but he's getting there."

"And what about Chen? Do you have a direct line of communication with him or are you dependent on picking up gossip?" Cutting rubbed the bridge of his nose and replaced his spectacles. They were new and he still wasn't used to them.

"I've met him face to face. An intriguing character, though I wouldn't trust him an inch. He's given me some useful historical background on the Commander – from their days in Hong Kong. You were there as well, weren't you sir?"

"I was indeed, Iain. Knew them both, but not well. Any information from that time has to be treated with caution. Rumour was king. Facts were a poor second."

The arrival of the silver tea service brought a natural break in the conversation. Cormack passed a slim file to Cutting, a summary of the Darkstone information to date and some material relating to Daid. Cutting thanked him. He could have used a more direct route to obtain the Darkstone details, but he wanted to deal with the issue at arm's length.

Cormack sipped his tea and resisted the temptation of a chocolate biscuit. He felt almost smug, but held this feeling in check, wondering again whether he was backing the right horse in this particular race.

December 23rd

"I've remembered who McPhee is?" Ellis cut another two slices of bread and put them in the toaster. Lorna looked puzzled.

"Who?"

"McPhee. You know the man Trawden mentioned. He said I should talk to him if I wanted to find out more about Rebecca. Well I couldn't sleep again last night and my mind was rambling all over the place. Then McPhee's face suddenly popped into my head. I remembered who he was. He bought some timber from me, for fencing work on his smallholding. He came here to pick it up and he wanted to see where it had been felled. I thought it was a little strange, but he said he always liked to know where his timber had been grown. So I took him up to the site. I'd been thinning out the saplings and told him I wouldn't be going back in there for a few years. He must have been checking which areas would be undisturbed, must have been planning the burial, just like that, cold-blooded. And of course it would have remained undisturbed had it not been for my wolf friend. I think we should pay Mr McPhee a visit."

"We?"

"Yes, if you're up for it. It's always less confrontational if you're visited by a domesticated couple don't you think?"

Lorna smiled. "I suppose you're right. Where does he live?"

"Across the water as they say around here – the other side of Loch Airne. It's about forty miles by road but we can use the boat.

And we don't need fuel coupons – it uses re-cycled cooking oil."

They left Toller in charge of Laska and with a small stand of trees to fell. He'd picked up the basics of using the chainsaw very quickly.

They walked to the boathouse under a clear sky, no wind to speak of, a perfect day to be on the water. Ellis rowed the boat out and pulled the cord on the elderly outboard motor. It took a few attempts before the engine finally coughed and spluttered into life. They steered north west, and watched the gulls fighting over the fish. They docked at a small jetty on the western shore of the loch. Ellis tied the boat up and they set off walking. McPhee's place was about two miles from the loch shore. It was a pleasant walk, hand in hand along a rough track.

Ellis spotted their man working in one of the fields, repairing a section of fencing and shouted a greeting, trying to sound as casual as possible. The man didn't recognise Ellis at first. When the light dawned he looked worried.

"I hope those posts are doing the job OK," Ellis called out. "Have you got a minute?" McPhee put down his hammer and walked slowly across to the field gate.

"Mr Landsman, sorry I didn't recognise you. What brings you over this side now?" He looked only at Ellis and ignored Lorna.

"Well it's a little difficult, but I was speaking to your man Mr Trawden the other day and he advised me to get in touch with you." McPhee seemed to shrink when he heard Trawden's name.

"The thing is, Mr McPhee, I found something on my land which Mr Trawden said you might know about."

McPhee leant suddenly against the gatepost, his face pale. He picked at a loose sliver of wood and for a moment gave this small task his complete attention. Ellis waited. Eventually McPhee turned to face away from them and looked towards the loch in the distance.

"Now I know nothing about this. All I'd say is that if I had been involved – which I wasn't, I'd have carried out the final piece of work and nothing else. Call it a disposal service if you like. The merchandise is delivered and my task would have been to dispose of it in an appropriate manner."

"And how would you have transported the merchandise to its final position?" Ellis asked.

"Oh, the same way you got here no doubt. For one thing it's a cheap way of travelling and for another you can arrive very quietly, especially when there's an easterly blowing, if you know what I mean."

"And you'd have had some help no doubt?"

"Two man job, two man job."

"So if we wanted to find out about how the merchandise ended up in its final condition, how would we go about doing that?" The question came from Lorna. She didn't want to be just a silent witness.

McPhee stared at her. Perhaps he was trying to work out whether he could answer her directly. He concluded that he could – perhaps because she was joining the conversation in the right spirit.

"Well, Miss, the only person I know who has any knowledge of this affair is the gentleman Mr Landsman mentioned in his first question. That and a whisper I heard about the Brig having a finger in the pie. Maybe they had an interest in the disappearance of the merchandise. That's about all I can say." McPhee wandered slowly back to where he had been working. The interview was over.

The sun continued to shine on their return trip, but the wind had picked up. Lorna found she could cope with the boat's rocking movement. She was a first time sailor, surprised at how she enjoyed their progress over the choppy loch waters. Maybe they could take the boat out again, just for fun.

McPhee stopped work again. He reached into his pocket for his phone.

"Yes, Landsman and some woman, don't know who she is. I told him just what you said I should – no more and no less."

December 26th

Ellis, Lorna and Toller had eaten themselves silly on Christmas Day. They'd sat by the fire in the evening getting slowly sozzled. Ellis rose late on Boxing Day and left for Glasgow without breakfast. Tom Cavanagh had phoned to tell him he'd found some information about Rebecca. Ellis travelled alone. Lorna was busy with translation work, aiming to bring in some money. They were running low on funds between them.

Cavanagh seemed pleased to see Ellis, but was clearly going downhill rapidly and had lost what little spark he'd had in the first place. He held some papers in his hands. Ellis asked him what they were. Cavanagh rubbed his eyes and scratched at his arm as he began speaking.

"She had this little hidey-hole under the floor boards in the bedroom. I only came across it by accident. She must have been keeping a diary of some sort, although it reads more like a book, as though she's looking on but not really involved. She was something of a writer in her own way and a bit of a poet. Look, this is the bit I think you should see."

He handed the handwritten sheets over to Ellis. It was written in green biro on cheap lined paper, but it was clear enough to read.

The clerk behind the reception desk wore a khaki shirt and tracksuit bottoms and was unshaven and red-eyed. He gestured to the guests to sign the register. Well they'd be guests for an hour or two anyway. The man scribbled something on the page and left three

twenties on the counter. Of course guests are supposed to produce
ID – in case the Brigade come checking – but the clerk didn't ask for
any. Perhaps something had been sorted out earlier. And in any
event, there was only one reason why guests visited these premises –
one that the Brig would not be that interested in, except perhaps for
blackmailing purposes.

The couple made their way up to the third floor and entered a
room which looked out over a busy street. He seemed to like the
atmosphere, but she felt it was sterile and somehow troubling. She
could see a flickering neon light through the net curtain. The large
double bed was covered in a thin duvet which the man pulled onto
the floor. He said he preferred the floor to the bed. There was a spare
blanket on the shelf in the wardrobe and he laid this over the duvet.

He told the woman his name was Hansen and he placed a small
bag of white powder on the glass-topped table in the corner of the
room, explaining that this was the form of payment he used. The
woman nodded and started to undress. He looked on, but made no
move to take off his own clothes. She pulled the duvet up around her.
There was no spare flesh on her but he seemed to be attracted by her
body. He eventually removed his trousers and joined her under the
duvet. To start with, they lay still. She looking up at the ornate
plasterwork of the ceiling rose and wondered how it had survived
all the changes. As he closed his eyes, she went to work.

When it was over, he got up immediately, put his clothes on and
started to flick through the Gideon Bible that was on the bedside
cabinet. Half-dressed, she stooped over the table, the powder in neat
lines. Once it was gone she sat on the edge of the bed and gazed
towards the window.

He wiped the top of the table with a tissue which he placed in a
small plastic bag, put the duvet back on the bed and returned the blanket
to the wardrobe. He glanced out of the window. She thought he was
checking that the 4x4 was still there on the opposite side of the street.

He asked her name and she told him. They arranged for the same time the following week. She felt he displayed a strange mixture of sadness and danger.

Ellis finished reading and looked at Tom Cavanagh who had tears in his eyes.

"It's part of a longer piece Bex was writing, keeping a record but turning her experiences into fiction. Maybe that was her way of coping with things. It's hard for me to read it – she had quite a tough life really. I've looked through all of it and the Hansen character makes a number of appearances. I can't prove it at all, but I think she may have died of an overdose or maybe took something that was contaminated. I think this man might have had something to do with it. She had a peculiar fascination with him. There's one reference to Trawden and Hansen together, so I was wondering whether you could go and see him again. I mean I'm really grateful for what you've done already, but I know Trawden would never give me the time of day and to be honest I don't think I could handle it."

Ellis didn't want to see Trawden again, but he knew it was his only way forward.

"Yes I can do that Tom. I'm not sure what I'll be able to get out of him. I might need some dirt on him first that I can use as leverage. I don't suppose you have anything do you?" He was met with a shake of the head.

* December 27th

Definitely the strangest Christmas I've ever had.

First off, the business with the Commander. I've started supplying him with info and I haven't told C yet. I can't decide whether to tell him or not. I haven't seen Daid since our meeting in the Biarritz, which is a relief because I don't want the creep anywhere near me.

Secondly it was so odd not being with Aran. At least I was able to phone her and we had a good long natter. She said that someone had spoken to mother and that she understood that I wouldn't be able to see them over Xmas. Aran seems to have had a bit of contact with the Brig one way or another.

But the strangest thing was when Lemmy contacted me out of the blue. My suspicions about him were right. He is Brig – goes under the name of Victor Charlesworth – and not only that, he's working on Darkstone!! He's the man on the outside and he's reporting to C just like me. We're not supposed to have any contact with each other. He was the one who had the real shock though. He'd found out that somebody had started work in Spook Central at the same time he'd been taken on out in the field. He had a feeling that the insider might have the same undercover remit as him. I don't know where he gets his info from but he was waiting for me yesterday evening. He'd tailed me from the office when I was on my way home. Except of course he didn't know it was me. He just knew I was one of the inside agents. He did this sort of double take when he saw me, like he knew *he knew me, but couldn't think who I was. I put him out of his misery and we walked back to my temporary home! He was really thrown. He'd been told I was dead and had been blaming himself for talking to me about Darkstone. He thought that had put me in danger. I kept on having to reassure him that it really was me.*

We had some catching up to do and some notes to swap. I thought very carefully about it and then decided to tell him about Daid and the information I was providing for him. We sat there wondering why he'd want his own supply of information, why he didn't appear to trust C – his own man. We chewed over the best way forward. My feeling was that we should keep our heads down at least for the time being. But Lemmy thought we should arrange to see C together. He didn't seem to be at all bothered about having broken all the rules in contacting me in the first place. He has some confidence that man. When he left he gave me a big hug. I have to say it felt really good. I don't think I'd have refused if he'd asked to stay! Maybe I'm just missing Aran.

December 28th

Ellis was worried about the kind of information he was unearthing. He needed to speak to Ross again. He didn't trust using his phone as he thought it would probably have a trace on it. And the mobile he'd been sent through the post only took incoming calls. But as far as he was aware, the Brigade didn't know anything about Lorna and she was happy for him to use her mobile.

"Hi there Ross, it's me. It would be good to meet up. Could you make it today?"

"Yes I've got a little free time. Where and when?"

"At noon, in the car park at the start of my father's favourite walk? You remember?"

"That'll do nicely. I always enjoyed that walk."

Ellis liked short phone conversations. The venue was a walk his father had been fond of, along the Clyde, near Cardross. Ross knew the score. Ellis thought he could spare just enough fuel for the return journey. They met up in a small car park overlooking the estuary.

The sky was steel grey and there was a strong easterly wind again. As Laska ran along the foreshore, Ellis did the introductions.

"Good to meet you Lorna. You've got a tough nut to crack here though," Ross said, putting his arm round Ellis' shoulder. "How's the search for Rebecca been going?"

"Your texts have been great, we're making progress." Ellis was upbeat but Ross looked puzzled.

"You've lost me, Ellis. What texts?"

"Oh Christ – it wasn't you who sent me the phone? Who the hell's been sending the texts then?" Ellis explained to his friend what had been happening. Ross looked concerned.

"So you've been getting some kind of inside information about what led to Rebecca's death?"

"Exactly! I thought it was you feeding us the details as your sleuthing progressed. Who else could be involved?"

"I've really no idea, but it sounds like someone in the Brigade has got a vested interest in you tracking down Rebecca's killer. What have you found out so far?"

"Well, I know who buried her and why he chose that particular part of my land – a guy called McPhee. From what I can work out, he acts as a clear-up man for William Trawden who…"

"Oh God not Billy Trawden!" Ross looked worried. "There's not much that he's not involved in – Mr Teflon, though, when it comes to convictions. The word is that he's got high level protection, as long as he doesn't stray too much from his mainstream activities. You need to be very careful if you're dealing with him."

Ellis didn't really want to hear this. He tried to focus on the practicalities. He asked Ross if there was any dirt on Trawden that he could use as leverage.

"I'll see what I can find. It'll be worth waiting a bit before you meet him, to give me a chance to find something juicy. You don't want to go in unarmed. He's a nasty piece of work. Keeps his own hands clean of course but he's got a number of very unsavoury assistants who aren't at all squeamish."

"Thanks for the warning. What you been up to yourself?"

"Ah, all pretty run of the mill stuff unfortunately." Ross was careful to say nothing about his continuing enquiries about Carla Lucini and Aran Caulfield. He could almost feel Cormack breathing down his neck.

They walked further along the shore. Ellis threw the ball time and again for Laska to chase, whilst Ross and Lorna followed on slowly behind, talking as if they were old friends. A steam launch puttered past, people sat at tables inside, eating and drinking, the sound of anodyne pop music drifted intermittently across the water. On the opposite bank, the urban sprawl of Greenock rose up, grey and forbidding.

"You were a Morton fan weren't you, Ross?" Ellis called out.

"Still am, still am, much good may it do me."

"Look, there's something I think I ought to tell you about. It's been worrying me. Have you ever come across a unit called Darkstone?"

Ross shook his head. Ellis told him about Lemmy, about the meeting they'd had and what they'd discussed.

"And Lemmy had given the same information to Carla. I just wondered whether it had anything to do with her death. I didn't tell you before because I thought it might compromise you. But now I think it would be safer if you knew about it."

"I've never heard of Darkstone," Ross said, "but thanks for the heads-up. I can check it out. But, if I were you, I wouldn't mention this to anyone else."

December 30th

Ross came up trumps with dirt on Trawden, or rather Trawden's son Robbie. He spoke to Ellis on Lorna's phone and gave him the details. Robbie was apparently a chip off the old block and was already running some of the businesses in the Trawden empire. He'd failed to stop after a fatal road accident and his identity had been covered up. Ross guessed this was through some sort of deal with the local Brigade chief. Only they hadn't done a very effective job of hiding the evidence and Ross managed to piece the story together.

Ellis thought this information would serve his purposes nicely. It was time to pay Mr Trawden another visit. En route he called in at the Flowerpot. He hadn't been there for years, but he remembered its location clearly enough, on a run-down side street off Gallowgate. In the old days the man who ran the café always wore his slippers and a flat cap. Ellis wondered whether the man behind the counter might be his son. There seemed to be a family resemblance. He had a bobble hat and wore green crocs on his bare feet. He pushed a cup of instant coffee across the table towards Ellis, spilling some of the luke-warm, brown liquid into the saucer. He took the opportunity of being away from the counter to wield his dustpan and brush, sweeping up haphazardly discarded butt ends, crisp packets and betting slips.

Ellis stared at the poster on the wall advertising holiday bargains – a week in Ibiza, ten days in Malta – and yearned for some warmth. But he couldn't afford any of them. His business, such as it was, just about kept him going but there was never any money for extras. A man in a long scarf and a flying helmet came into the café and hovered behind Ellis' seat, breathing heavily, his cough a frequent, rasping, rattle. He didn't say a word before moving off to a seat in the corner to slurp noisily at his mug of tea.

Ellis slowly realised that his cup was empty, yet he couldn't remember drinking the coffee. He'd been trying to eke it out. He drummed his fingers on the café table and contemplated ordering another drink. The tinkling of the bell on the café door announced Lorna's arrival. She'd been visiting an elderly aunt, dropping off food and medicine, running round with the vacuum and clearing out the empties.

Lorna waved and stepped back outside again. The café wasn't her sort of place. Ellis paid up and left. They walked together to Central Station. As they crossed the main concourse, something about the man just ahead of them caught Ellis' attention. He looked familiar – tall, broad, with a slightly loping gait. Where had he seen him before? It suddenly came to him.

"Lemmy," he called out. The man seemed to hesitate slightly and then carry on walking. Ellis quickened his pace, overtook him and then turned to look back. He was right – it was Lemmy. For an instant his man's face displayed a mixture of embarrassment and annoyance and then softened into a look of recognition.

"It's Ellis isn't it? Well, well – what a pleasant surprise." He caught sight of Lorna out of the corner of his eye. "Sorry, is this a friend of yours?" Lorna approached and shook hands.

"Yes, I'm Ellis' new girlfriend." She picked up from Ellis' look that it would be better if she made herself scarce for a while. "I'm just going to get our train tickets. Nice to meet you, Lemmy."

"Very nice, Ellis! You're a lucky man. By the way how's the search going?"

Ellis wasn't quite sure how much – or how little – to tell him. "I seem to have come up against a series of brick walls. As an amateur outsider it's pretty clear I'm not going to get far. Maybe you could help."

"In what way?"

"Well, you were probably one of the last people to see Carla. Is there anything else you can think of that might help me in my search – any little thing she might have said or done that you perhaps hadn't remembered when we met before?"

In his turn, Lemmy was unsure how much to tell Ellis Landsman.

"I've been over it in my mind it time and again. There's nothing, which is a shame because I really liked the lassie. It's probably grasping at straws and it'll be a bit of a shock to you, but I've heard a whisper that she might not actually be dead, that the Brig might have done a body switch for some reason."

Ellis wasn't surprised to hear about the body switch – but wasn't prepared for the news that Carla might not actually be dead.

"Whoah! I think you've lost me there, Lemmy. Can you rewind a bit?"

"Yeah – sorry. I can get a bit carried away. One of my contacts heard that Carla was a Brigade officer and might have been disappeared for some reason – you know, they pretend she's dead but she's really taken on a new identity."

Ellis gazed across the concourse towards three huge wheelie bins, garbage overflowing waiting for an endlessly postponed collection. There was a sudden deafening announcement, the usual warning about security, baggage and strangers, delivered at a volume that distorted the message completely.

"That's a hell of a lot to take in, all at once," Ellis said. "So I could have been wasting my time completely. Hang on though! Whose body did I find then?" He was fishing for information about Rebecca, but this time he was disappointed.

"Good question. Unfortunately I can't help you on that one. Don't take this stuff as gospel mind. My informants have been known to be wrong. But they are insiders."

"So how come they're willing to talk to you?"

"There's some of them don't like the Brig set up at all. They reckon it stinks. So – to the right person – they'll let out snippets of information and get them to put two and two together. But of course they have to be careful. A lot of their so-called colleagues are complete Cromwells – you know – total puritans."

Ellis wanted to make the most of his chance encounter. He decided to play the Darkstone card.

"Remember when we met up, you told me about some undercover project – Darkstone wasn't it?" Lemmy nodded. "Well have you picked up anything else about it in your travels?"

Again, Lemmy was unsure about how much information to pass on. He didn't want to put either Carla or himself at risk.

"As it happens, I've heard a couple of things." He pulled Ellis to one side and dropped his voice. "You'll have read about that train that was blown up. Awful business, a man called Meikle was behind it – a complete nutcase. Well apparently it's been carte blanche since then against the so-called opposition and it's being led by our friends in Darkstone. The second thing's a bit more hush hush. Their HQ was attacked – crazy thing to do. Nobody knows yet who was behind it, but it's just made it even worse for us. They're ramping it up into some sort of full blown terrorist attack, but from what I've heard there was minimal damage."

Ellis went pale. He was trying not to put two and two together. He didn't want to think about Toller attempting to blow up the Darkstone HQ. Maybe there had been more than one recent explosive attack in central Glasgow over the last few days. He knew he was fooling himself. Perhaps he'd need to talk to Toller.

"Are you OK Ellis? Are you coming down with something?"

"Well I have been a bit under the weather. But it's nothing." He regained his composure. Lemmy seemed nervous. He checked his watch. Ellis couldn't help noticing it was an expensive looking piece of work. It didn't seem to fit with the rest of his image. Ellis liked it when people surprised him in this way. He didn't even own a wristwatch. He looked up at the station clock and saw the huge minute hand click forward. He could see Lorna coming through the crowd, tickets in hand. Lemmy touched him on the shoulder.

"Time to go Ellis – sorry. Have to get back East and I'm running late already. Good to meet you again though. Here, take this, it's my new number," he said as he handed Ellis a business card. "Take care." With that, he was off, striding towards one of the far platforms.

"If we're quick we've just got time to catch the twenty past." Lorna shouted.

It was a rapid, smooth ride on the suburban electric. Nothing less would do for the well-heeled commuters of Milngavie. Ellis had arranged an appointment with Trawden this time. He'd refused at first but then Ellis dropped the son's name into the conversation. Lorna again insisted on accompanying Ellis. She asked him about the conversation with Lemmy. He told her the gist of it and tried to keep his voice as low as possible.

They splashed out on a taxi from the station up to Trawden's house, phoning beforehand to tell him they were about to arrive. The pedestrian gate was already open and a beefy looking man with a shaved head, wearing a suit that was slightly too small, led them round to a large conservatory at the rear of the property. Lorna could see that the man was trying to hold his stomach in. A snake's head tattoo emerged from the right hand cuff of his suit jacket. The man disappeared. They waited a few minutes. The room was pleasantly warm and full of plants. Trawden made his entry holding a watering can with a long spout and proceeded to drip water into the red clay pots, talking to his guests as he did so.

"Still on the trail then? What's this nonsense about Robbie?"

"25th October 6:00pm, Cambuslang, a hit and run on a crossing. Pedestrian didn't make it unfortunately. It seems that young Robbie had been on the bevvy. He made it as far as Farrar's garage where miraculously, by the time the police arrived, the vehicle had disappeared into thin air. They'd been rather conveniently delayed. And, lo and behold, when they checked the CCTV camera at the crossing, they found it hadn't been working."

"I hear what you're saying, Mr Landsman. But it's only fair to let you know that I have good insurance cover where it matters, which means that this rubbish you're spouting is never going to see the light of day. I'm sure you get my drift. Now if there's anything else I can help you two with?"

"Sorry it's not really that simple, Mr Trawden. You see, I happen to know that the camera was working and that there is a copy of the relevant footage. If that were to surface, it might not look so good for your son, not just the hit and run to think about, but the cover up. In my experience it's always the cover up where the mistakes are made."

Trawden had stopped his watering and was giving Landsman his full attention.

"I'm sure your influence with the police or the Brigade is next to non-existent young man. Nevertheless, there may be some scope for me to assist you a little. I understand you've spoken to McPhee and that he told you of a possible link between Leuchars and the Brigade. I can confirm that and I suggest that you focus your attention on the top floor of John Knox House. What I can also tell you is that the termination was nothing to do with McPhee. He simply carried out the disposal. It was just a matter of business, Mr Landsman."

"Was Rebecca on your payroll, Mr Trawden?" Lorna had become more and more frustrated with the conversation. They were talking about flesh and blood – a woman's life and her death. She remembered all too clearly what Tom Cavanagh had said about Trawden.

"Perhaps you should have left the girlfriend at home making the tea, Mr Landsman. I don't think she understands the rules of the game."

"On the contrary, Mr Trawden, I think she understands them all too well and reckons it's about time we cut the crap."

"Oh, such a shame and just when we were getting on so well. Of course information about my business activities is confidential, whether it's my clients or my associates. All I will say is that, having met her just the once, I'm not surprised that her life was a little foreshortened. Now if you'll forgive me I have an appointment with my accountant."

Trawden left the conservatory and the two of them sat staring vacantly through the double-glazed windows out to the lifeless garden. Ellis shrugged his shoulders.

"I suppose that's as much as we're going to get just now. I wonder where Baldy is?"

Right on cue their shaven-headed guide returned and led them silently through the garden and out through the pedestrian gate.

"What is John Knox House?" Lorna asked as they walked back to the station. The name rang a bell but she couldn't bring anything to mind.

"It's a name I'll never forget," Ellis said. "It's the Brigade HQ. It's where they took my father for interrogation. He was never the same after that, never recovered really."

Ellis had told Lorna a little about his father on previous occasions, but he usually clammed up after a few sentences. This time however, he went much further and talked about the good times as well. She hadn't realised that Kintrawe House had been in Ellis' family since the 1930's.

He told her how his grandfather had bought the property cheaply during the Depression and planted the woodlands. His father had taken over for a while, but had then lost interest, preferring the urban life and involvement in the politics that would eventually lead to his death. A local couple had rented the property for a few years, but when they decided to leave the newly designated Outlands area it had stood empty until Ellis had moved in. He'd welcomed the peace and isolation of the place, even though he could barely make a living there. Lorna was surprised that Ellis had suddenly opened up like this and hoped it wouldn't be just a one-off. She brought him back to the present.

"Do you think he'll be waiting for us?"

"Who?"

"Toller of course."

Toller had travelled in with them to the city that morning. He'd been suffering from cabin fever, missing the sights and sounds of Glasgow. They'd agreed to meet up at the station for the journey back, but they'd both had their doubts whether he'd be there. Toller had said he'd stay away from his estate, but neither of them believed this. The temptation to see his friends would be too great.

They waited an extra half an hour at the station, but there was no sign of him. They were silent on the journey home, both worried about what might have happened to Toller.

* January 2nd

Hogmanay was even more depressing than Christmas Day if that's possible. The rubbish on TV is unbelievable. Thank goodness the so-called holiday season is out of the way. I'm wondering how much more information we'll have to collect – me and Lemmy that is – before C or the boss decide to pull the plug on Darkstone.

We've come across three cases where it looks like an agent has eliminated a target – and not in self-defence. We think it must be officially sanctioned. The targets have all been pretty extreme dudes, but that doesn't justify their murder.

Then there are the disappearances – suspects being carted off to some sort of holding facility, God knows where.

We talked about the disappearances and the terminations and reckon we're just seeing the tip of the iceberg. We've picked up a lot in the short time we've been working for Darkstone, so the total amount of this extreme stuff over a longer period must be worryingly high.

On the run of the mill stuff, we've already got enough detail to sink a ship. So, how much more do they need and what are their real intentions? My old doubts are returning.

Lemmy and I discussed it last night at his flat. Well it's a bedsit not a flat really – just about enough room to swing a kitten. We agreed that C needs to be told. We mulled it over and decided it would be better not to tell him that we know about each other. There's no point in unnecessarily antagonising the man. So Lemmy's going to meet him on his own.

I need to talk to C anyway, but that will have to be at our next regular meeting. I'm going to tell him about Daid and ask him how much longer it will be before I can meet up with Aran. To be truthful I'm not actually missing her as much as I thought I would. Maybe it's the adrenaline from this job that's keeping me going.

January 3rd

Toller had been moving from house to house, keeping his hood up and his head down. Something had changed on the estate. Nobody said anything outright, but he felt as if they held him responsible for Dommo's death. Maybe not responsible – but at least partly to blame. *You knew he was a bampot – why did you take him along?*

Perhaps he was losing his taste for the lunatic fringe stuff on the estate. He had to admit he was missing the solitude of the woods. He needed to talk to someone.

When he called to see Colette she was out. Gam very reluctantly let him in and said he could wait. He sat silently in a corner of the living room while Gam tapped away at the keyboard, trying to ignore his unwanted visitor.

"Did you know that Ellis found a body in his woods?" Toller found himself blurting out.

"What?" Gam raised his head momentarily from the laptop. Toller explained. "Oh yes, he told us about that."

"Well it's not who he thought it was."

Gam wondered whether the lad was short of a few marbles, although Colette had told him how bright he was. Toller explained again. Gam was taken aback.

"So who was it?"

"Some druggie. Ellis is doing some digging. Billy Trawden's on his list. You know him?" Gam turned round to face Toller, who'd never seen him look so animated before.

"Trawden! Shit, Ellis better be careful or he'll end up as dog food."

"I think he knows the score. He's alright you know." Toller heard the front door slamming and Colette shouting a greeting to Gam. She looked worried when she came into the room and saw Toller.

"It's OK, I've just come for a chat, some advice like. I won't stay long."

The two of them went into the kitchen. Toller leaned against the worktop as Colette put the kettle on and cut a couple of slices of homemade cake.

"So, how's it going out there, Toller?"

He explained what had happened, told her he didn't know what to do. She talked to him slowly, reassuringly, asked him about the Outlands. He sounded enthusiastic, said he thought maybe he should go back, but wondered what they'd think, with him sneaking off like that.

"Why don't you ask them? I've got Lorna's number. Give her a ring."

He looked uncertain at first and then took a phone out of his pocket. "It's nicked so the Brig won't know it's mine. That's if they're checking."

He dialled the number that Colette had scribbled on a scrap of paper and waited. He was slow to respond when the call was answered. This was the first proper conversation he'd had with Lorna. "Hi, it's me…er yes, that's right. Sorry about not being there the other day. I had to go home. Well not home exactly, but you know what I mean. What? Oh yes I do, that's why I'm phoning. I'm at Colette's. She said I should call. The thing is I'm a bit embarrassed about skipping. I didn't know what you would think about me coming back. What? Oh that's great. Can you pick me up from near the station – that lay-by? Awesome. I'll give you a ring."

He put the phone in his pocket and hugged Colette. This was the first time she'd ever seen him show any signs of emotion.

"I was telling Gam about what Ellis has been doing. I'm wondering whether he needs any help, you know, with information and such like. I mean Gam knows a lot of stuff, he'll have the connections no doubt. Perhaps you could talk to your man about helping Ellis out."

"I think you're right, Toller. I'll talk to him about it. So you're getting on alright with Ellis then?"

"Aye. I thought he was a bit of a weirdo at first, but I like all the forest work, the chainsaw and that and the dog. He's a real friend."

"And what about Dommo? Are you getting dreams?"

Toller struggled to hold it together. "Every night, every fucking night. Sorry Colette." She hugged him again.

+ + +

Ellis was using his artistic skills to try and piece together the events that had led to Rebecca's death.

He laid out several pieces of paper on the kitchen table. On the first one he'd drawn a rough sketch of Rebecca and Tom Cavanagh together and placed it on the top left hand corner of the table, just over the burn mark where he'd absent-mindedly placed a hot casserole dish straight from the oven a few years ago. Then he drew portraits of William Trawden and whatsisname McPhee. What was his first name? He realised he didn't know. His final portrait would be of Hansen, the man Rebecca had described in her writing. He was convinced Hansen was involved in some way in Rebecca's death. He might also be the man that Trawden had referred to, the one from the top floor of John Knox House. So, who occupied the top floor these days? Was it still the bosses?

Until he had the answer, the portrait would have to remain faceless with a big H in the middle of it.

Lorna brought him a cup of tea and stared at the sketches on the table.

"What's this all about, Ellis – a new game?"

"I suppose it is in a way. The idea is to join the dots that link these characters together. I mean we know where some of the dots go, but what's the real link between Trawden and Hansen? Is Hansen the killer? Or maybe he allowed the death to happen. And why would he use Trawden to finish off his dirty work? It seems a very risky route – open to blackmail and who knows what. We're lacking any proof though."

"Maybe you need to draw him out – Hansen I mean," Lorna said. "It could be dangerous but why not invite him round and put your cards on the table – literally." She scanned the portraits lined up on the table.

Ellis looked intrigued and then frowned, "Yes, I realise we don't know who Hansen is – not yet. But if he's top floor that narrows it down. I need to speak to Ross."

"Maybe, but don't forget we've only got Trawden's word for all this. He's bound to have a strong interest in throwing us off the trail or framing someone who's not actually the killer at all."

"You're right to be cautious, but the word on the street is that Trawden only deals with the top men. You heard him talk about his insurance policy. Did you see the look on his face when he said that? It was a mix of superiority and smugness. *I deal only with the big guys.* Anyway – what have we got to lose?"

"A great deal if what everyone keeps telling us about Trawden is true. Even Toller knows the score with that man." Lorna clasped her hands anxiously.

"You're right – again. But I've got to do something. I feel we're just on the edge of cracking this. I can't give up now."

Lorna looked at him. "I can see I'm not going to change your mind. Here – give Ross a ring, see what he knows." She handed Ellis her phone. "I hope he's made some progress tracking down our mysterious texter. It must be someone in the Brigade, surely and someone who's well informed."

Ellis took the phone and paused to stare again at the portraits, as if willing them to tell him some vital piece of information.

"Thanks. I just hope Ross will still want to play. The stakes are getting higher and he's got his family to think of. But I have to try. He could come here. The Brigade know we're in contact anyway."

He dialled the number and waited while the phone rang. He began to feel worried, threatened almost. It wasn't one specific threat, just a general sense of foreboding.

January 4th

When Ross got back to the office after his trip to Kintrawe House he sat for a while trying to make sense of what was happening. Ellis wanted him to help identify the person who'd killed Rebecca Leuchars. He suspected it was a man who went under the name of Hansen who was, in all likelihood, one of the Brigade's top brass. Ross was completely out of his depth. A simple favour for an old friend had come back to haunt him. His leverage, the things he'd found out about Aran Caulfield and Carla Lucini now seemed almost trivial to him. He didn't want to be sucked in any further.

He had two options. He could do nothing, stop responding to Ellis' requests and hope that everything would go away. He pictured himself as a seven year old, pulling the bedclothes over his head, hoping the sound of his parents' arguments would stop. Or he could go to confession again with 'Father' Cormack. It might even be to his benefit, providing information that would be of assistance to the Brigade. He was only too familiar, though, with the usual fate of whistleblowers. The first person to be shot was generally the original bearer of bad news, no matter how things turned out subsequently.

It took him only a couple of minutes to conclude that doing nothing was not really an option. He picked up his phone and called Cormack. To his surprise he was told to come straight to the Major's office. He had no time to decide whether this immediate access was a good or a bad sign.

Cormack sat behind a large highly polished desk which was completely empty apart from a marble sculpture of an elephant. Ross wondered, momentarily, whether this had any significance. Cormack had his elbows on the desk and his hands placed together in a steeple.

"Well, Sergeant, what have you got for me this time, something useful I hope?" It took a while before a response was forthcoming.

"I'm sorry Major, but could I possibly have a glass of water?" Ross was almost croaking.

Cormack fetched him a bottle of spring water from the fridge in the corner of the office and placed a crystal glass on the wide arm of the seat. "Take your time. I appreciate you will be nervous."

The water helped and it gave Ross time to gather his thoughts. "This is all very awkward, sir." He explained what Ellis Landsman had worked out. "You see, he suspects that one of the people involved in Rebecca Leuchars' death is from John Knox House."

Cormack nodded briefly. "And I assume he's not suggesting it was one of the cleaners there!"

"No sir. Sorry, he's convinced it's a senior Brigade office, perhaps very senior."

"I see. Perhaps you can give me a little more detail, so I've got something more substantial to get my teeth into."

Ross gave him chapter and verse, insofar as he was aware of it. Cormack rose from his seat and walked across to the window. He spoke without looking at Ross.

"You've done the right thing coming to me, Lambert. You will of course be fully aware that this is highly sensitive material and you must tell nobody what you have told me, absolutely nobody. Is that clear?"

"It's very clear, Major. Might I ask what will happen next?"

"I think it would be better if you knew as little as possible about what happens next, don't you? All I will say is that you should have no further contact with Landsman until I tell you. I'll arrange for him to be dealt with directly. Now is that all Sergeant?"

Ross hesitated. He wanted to ask Cormack about the mystery mobile, the one that was being used to provide key pieces of information to Ellis. But he couldn't bring himself to ask the question. Maybe it wasn't really that important now. He shook his head, thanked the Major and left the office.

As he walked down the stairs to the ground floor he reflected on the interview. He thought it strange that Cormack hadn't appeared to be surprised by anything he'd been told. He hadn't got heated, hadn't issued any threats and hadn't given the usual speech about the honour of the Brigade. He'd just nodded calmly like he'd been told about the duty roster for the following week. Why had he been so calm? Unless of course he already knew about Hansen.

January 5th

His plans were coming to fruition and Cormack wanted to savour the moment. His operatives providing all the information he needed about Darkstone. Pelham, who he'd never trusted, was out of the picture. Landsman was coming up trumps, helped by a little prompting from himself and Daid was ripe for the plucking. Of course Daid was his own worst enemy, unable to keep his trousers on and unable to cover the tracks left by his size twelve boots.

When Garside had told him the name of the woman who'd been found dead in an Outland forest, Cormack hadn't been able to believe his luck. He already knew the name Rebecca Leuchars. It had surfaced previously during an enquiry he'd led into William Trawden's activities. But he'd also found a reference to Leuchars in one of Daid's notebooks. He'd been left alone, briefly, in the Commander's office and had taken the opportunity to flick through the notes. Daid's spidery handwriting was difficult to read, but Cormack had just sufficient time to pick up two references to Leuchars. He could never understand why people who should know better insisted on keeping written records of potentially incriminating information. The co-incidental occurrences of the name had set him thinking and had led to the idea of using Landsman as his unwitting detective. He calculated that an unsophisticated outsider would be able to make more progress in this delicate area than his own professionals.

Given the information he'd had from Lambert it now only

remained for Daid to incriminate himself and with what Cormack had in mind, that would happen very soon.

His moment of euphoria was short-lived. His phone rang. He looked at the screen. It was Charlesworth. He thought for a moment. Did he really want any grief this late at night? But his responsible, organised, efficient self took over and he spoke to his agent.

"I thought I told you this number was for emergencies only. This had better be one!"

"It depends how you define an emergency Major Cormack. We need to talk."

"What about?"

"I think this would be better done face to face."

Lemmy sounded firm, measured and almost, but not quite, threatening. Cormack made a quick decision. From what he knew of the agent, he wasn't one to cry wolf. He had his suspicions about him, about the man's real agenda, but he was certainly experienced and never one to panic.

"OK, but I can't see you until next week. It'll be the 7th, 7:30am, Ferguson Building." He hung up.

Cormack was livid. He was the one who controlled events – they didn't control him. What did the agent want, what had he found out? Maybe he should have been more cautious about appointing Charlesworth with his track record.

Cormack tried to put this particular problem to the back of his mind. His calm returned and he thought with pleasure of another meeting – the one he was just about to arrange with his boss.

* January 5th

I can't decide whether to think of him as Victor or Lemmy. I wonder what his real name is. Perhaps even he can't remember. He left me a message to say he'd set up the meeting with C. I didn't know Ferguson House was one of ours. Maybe it isn't.

We got details of another termination today. Of course it was described as a self defence response to an extreme hostile situation, but there'll be no external investigation. Some of our guys are effectively turning into licensed killers. There'll be an internal panel hearing, where any probing questions will be kept to a minimum and the 'victim' will be cast as someone involved in terrorism, who our brave boys have been tracking for weeks or months. But from a quick scan of the circumstances I'd say that in the four cases I've now come across, the targets have been oppositionists for sure, but by no stretch of the imagination could they be described as terrorists. There've been a couple more cases where people have disappeared. Sounds odd me saying that. I wonder who has authorised this rendition programme. I mean, that's what it is. Scotland's only a small country with no real recent history of terrorist activity, but you wouldn't think so looking at the publicity that spews out of the SecureScotland machine. And because of the volume of low grade activity we're monitoring, there's always a danger we'd miss the real thing if it happened.

Anyway, enough of that. I eventually plucked up the courage to tell C about Daid. It was a real anti-climax. He claimed he knew all about it. I'm sure there's more to this than meets the eye, but I know C won't tell me any more. Still, on the plus side he said I could meet up with Aran at last. Can't wait for tomorrow.

January 6th

The phone vibrated – an incoming text. *Kelvingrove Museum 11:00 a.m.* Charles Daid stared at the small screen and wondered what Cormack wanted. He only ever texted like this when it was something important, something urgent. He asked Moira to arrange the car for 10:30 and waited impatiently for the time to pass. He couldn't concentrate.

He'd started getting these long, tiring dreams, a Pelham-like figure endlessly following him. However hard he tried he couldn't seem to shake him off. Occasionally the figure would become clearer and he could see that it wasn't Pelham at all. He'd wake, exhausted.

The buzzer sounded, signalling the car's arrival. It took fifteen minutes to reach the museum. Cormack was already there sitting in a corner of the café with two coffees in front of him. Daid thought something about him looked different. He'd always had that inner confidence, but now it was almost a look of superiority.

The two men shook hands. Cormack pushed a large envelope across the table towards his boss and adjusted his spectacles. Daid noticed they were new. The fashion had swung back to small frames. He didn't like them. He opened the envelope and pulled out several closely-typed sheets of paper which summarised Darkstone's activity over the last month. He scanned the pages quickly. He knew the detail already. The Lucini woman had provided it. He was impatient to know what Cormack really wanted.

"Good work Iain. We can use this very profitably. I'll fix a meeting with Brigadier Cutting and raise the issue of this extra-curricular activity. We'll see if Morrisey can defend the indefensible. Then we'll be in a position to take over, clean up and run the place our way."

Cormack nodded, pushed the papers back in the envelope and took a sip of his cappuccino.

"So you'd keep Darkstone going then?"

"Of course, it's far too valuable to close down. It just needs to be reined in a little and integrated into our structure. Morrisey needs to be pensioned off and we both know who'll be best placed to take over." It was almost a smile, but not quite.

Cormack took another sip of his coffee. "There was one other item." He was enjoying himself. "It's a bit tricky. It's about the body that Landsman found – the one that wasn't Carla Lucini."

Daid looked bored and annoyed. Had Cormack dragged him out to the museum just to give him unwanted details about some unimportant dead woman?

"Is this really necessary? Can't it wait till our regular meeting?"

"I don't think so," Cormack continued. "You see it's a little personal, Commander. Her name was Rebecca Leuchars."

Daid was silent and betrayed no sign of recognising the name.

"She was an addict and a call girl." Cormack used the phrase deliberately. He thought it had a nice old-fashioned ring to it. "Well the two went together really. The thing is I've received some information which indicates that you may have known her." Cormack had to hand it to his boss. He was good, no give-away movements, not even a flicker. Cormack thought for a dreadful moment that maybe his information might be wrong. But he'd done the necessary checking and cross-checking. He knew he was right.

"And what?" was all Daid said.

"Well, there are some er…" Cormack hesitated, "…accusations, about her suppliers. She claimed that you were one of them. Now I know that's an outlandish claim, but obviously we need to be able to repudiate it."

A middle-aged couple moved towards an adjacent table and prepared to sit down. Their introductory half smiles were met with a stony look from Cormack and they moved hastily to the other side of the sparsely occupied café.

"Where did your evidence come from?"

"From Landsman. He's a lot more adept at this sort of thing then we thought. Of course, we'd no reason to think he was operating in sensitive territory. We didn't know about all the complications Ms Leuchars had in her short, troubled life. Landsman wants to talk to you, at his house out in the sticks. I imagine he's got some sort of deal in mind." Cormack looked straight at his boss. "You may need to take some precautionary measures. Of course it's up to you, sir." He emphasised the word *sir*. He could almost feel a transfer of power taking place.

"Tell him I'll be there. Let's get it over with. I can't have a man like him spouting such drivel. The sooner he knows the true position the better. I'll drive up there myself. Can't remember the last time I was in the Outlands. And your suggestion of some precautions is a good one, just in case things turn awkward. Can you arrange that and let me have the necessary?"

Cormack pulled a small box from his briefcase and handed it to Daid. "Here's something I had prepared earlier sir," he said.

Daid was both impressed by the man's efficiency and worried by his soulless concentration. He took the box and carried it as if it were a bomb. He walked across the heavily polished marble floor, his heels clicking with each step.

Cormack chuckled and ordered another coffee and an extra-large piece of coffee and walnut cake. A refrain from the distant past ran through his mind – *"Will you come into my parlour said the spider to the fly..."*

+ + +

Ellis and Toller were felling a stand of trees. Toller had proved to be a quick learner and was already adept at operating the chainsaw. Ellis had guessed, rightly, that the power of the machine would appeal to him.

Toller had struggled at first to cope with Kintrawe's isolation and Ellis had been surprised when he'd returned after his brief city-break. Toller had told him that he'd realised there wasn't a whole lot to go back to. His mates were there and their daily activities held some attractions, but it wasn't enough. He was only sixteen when his father had died from liver failure. Things had got more difficult after that and in the end, his mother had kicked him out, claiming rightly that she could no longer control him. He saw his two elder brothers from time to time but they were inside more often than not. Toller had so far managed to keep out of prison, but he felt he'd be pushing his luck if he continued to live on the estate. And of course there was the little matter of his involvement in that underground explosion. Out in the forest he felt a long way from the Brigade's tentacles.

The saw cut effortlessly into the pine and the tree fell with a muffled thump into the powdery snow. They stopped for a smoke and a drink of tea. Ellis felt the mystery phone vibrating in his pocket. He pulled it out. *The top man is on his way, take care.* So Ross had passed his message on. He'd had some doubts about whether he would. He'd guessed that Ross would be in two minds about involving himself in accusations about one of his most senior officers. He still hadn't been told the name of the man. But he wouldn't have to wait much longer to find out.

It was time to pack up and walk the horse back to the house. The animal dragged two large tree trunks along through the snow. The smaller pieces had been stacked for later collection. Ellis could see Lucas the wolf shadowing them through the trees. He thought he looked thinner than usual, almost forlorn. Ellis said nothing. He didn't want Toller to go chasing after him.

Ellis had made a temporary stable in one of the old sheds and Toller led the horse into the building and filled the old manger with hay.

Lorna asked Ellis how the felling had gone. They sat eating at the kitchen table, but Toller was not one for mealtime conversation and he left to return to the bunk house as soon as he'd finished. Lorna breathed a sigh of relief.

"Doesn't get any easier does it?" Ellis helped himself to more carrots.

"I think he's getting better, opening up more than he used to. Oh and we've got a visitor on the way."

"The mysterious Mr Hansen?"

"The man himself. I've been told to take care. He won't know about you or Toller so you both better disappear. Toller can sort the sheep out but if you can keep an ear open from upstairs, that would be great."

+ + +

Charles Daid was finding it difficult to see through the large powdery snowflakes. For the last half hour he'd encountered no other traffic.

He'd been reflecting on his weakness. It had always been sex, from those early days in Hong Kong, the achingly attractive women in their slit skirts, through to his current addiction for backstreet hotels. Bex had been a favourite. She'd asked for the cocaine when her usual supplier had cut her off and he'd provided it. But she'd got greedy and he knew things were getting too risky. She'd somehow discovered his real identity. He must have been really careless. She said she wanted money or else she'd have to tell someone about his habits – supplying and using. He'd called Trawden. All it had taken was a contaminated dose and a rapid disposal far from the city.

He and Trawden understood each other. Each could bring the other down but neither had any real motive to do so. They referred to it jokingly as their policy of Mutually Assured Destruction and it had worked so far.

Daid's mind was drifting and he nearly missed the left turning to Landsman's place. He had to reverse through the rapidly settling snow. There were no lights in sight, just endless trees and the occasional clearing. At one point he thought the track had given out but it had just narrowed. The 4x4 bounced over the ruts.

At last he saw a single light at the end of the track. He pulled the vehicle up in front of a wood store and stepped out into the yard, bottle in hand. The door to the house opened and a tall man peered out and beckoned him in.

"I'm afraid I don't know your name."

"It's Daid. You must be Landsman." A nod. "A little something to warm us up." Daid handed over the single malt and they walked inside. Laska stirred momentarily and then resumed his prone position in front of the fire.

"You're well settled here, I see. I'm not surprised you didn't really stir for – what was it – nearly ten years. Glasses?"

Ellis produced two small crystal glasses and poured out generous measures. They sat silently for a moment savouring the first taste.

"So you've been checking up on me, I hear?" Daid said.

"Well the body has become something of a fixation. The

change of identity made no difference. I needed to know who it was, and why my forest had been used as a graveyard." Ellis was getting into his stride. "I mean it's never happened to me before. I've never been a great believer in co-incidence up until now. Or is it fate, or destiny? You probably haven't heard of Mr McPhee."

Daid shook his head. He was rolling the malt around his mouth, trying to hold on to the exquisite taste.

"It was funny really," Ellis continued. "He was one of my customers, came for a whole pile of fence posts, old wagon, I didn't think it would get across the yard, let alone make it back to the other side of the loch. I took him to the copse where the posts had come from, showed him where I was felling and where I'd finished. For some reason he seemed interested. Turns out of course the bastard was surveying for a suitable burial ground, somewhere that would be undisturbed. And, as you no doubt know, it would have stayed that way had it not been for the intervention of Lucas."

"Why don't you get to the point son?" Ellis had been concentrating on telling his story and hadn't noticed his father's arrival on the scene.

"Because I'm in no hurry. I want to build up to a climax gradually."

"I know this guy. He interviewed me once, not long before the end. He was OK, not like the others."

"What, so I'm supposed to go easy on him?"

"No, I'm just giving you some background, some perspective."

"You were saying, Mr Landsman. Who is this Lucas guy?"

"He's a wolf."

Daid stopped drinking momentarily. This was weird. Why hadn't Cormack told him anything about a wolf?

Ellis glanced up and continued, "He was the one who found the body. Probably hadn't eaten in a long while. So that scuppered Mr McPhee's carefully laid plans. But then of course the higher powers decided they wanted to use the body to help Ms Lucini disappear and then reappear in a new guise." Ellis hoped that Lemmy's intuition on this point was right. "You'll know all about that. Something to eat?"

Daid nodded and Ellis went to the kitchen. Daid moved swiftly and unscrewed the top off a small bottle he produced from his jacket pocket. He poured a few drops of a colourless liquid into Ellis' whisky. Daid knew it was also tasteless and traceless, perfect for his intentions. Task completed, he stood and looked at the unframed paintings pinned to the wall opposite the fireplace. He thought the one featuring the wolf was really very good, got the essence of the creature, there and not there.

Ellis returned from the kitchen and placed some small plates on the table, cheese, crackers, slices of cold curried rabbit, home-made plum chutney.

"I was just admiring the picture of the wolf. Yours by any chance?" Ellis nodded. "That's quite a skill. Do you sell them?"

"I sell some. Others I prefer to keep." Ellis picked up his whisky. "I spoke to Mr McPhee recently. After a little persuasion he put me onto a friend of yours, a Mr Trawden. Not a helpful man, but we reached an accommodation in the end. He seemed to come to a conclusion that he had more to lose from disappointing me than he had from disappointing you. Strange really – I didn't think I had that much power. Of course it would be his word against yours at the end of the day and I think we know who would win that particular contest. But Mr Trawden is not the only witness for the prosecution so to speak. As luck would have it, Ms Leuchars was something of a writer and you were one of her main characters. It's not the sort of evidence that would stand up in a court of law, but I found it very convincing.

"Now you and I both know this case is never going to get to court but that's never been my intention. My aim is to aid your retirement, preferably without your no doubt excessive pension. To put it bluntly – to see you gone. What do you say?"

For the first time, Daid looked uncertain of himself. "You are very similar to your father. You won't know this but I had the pleasure – and it was a pleasure – of interviewing him. You're dogged and determined, but, to use an expression I think you'll like – you can't see the wood for the trees. What makes you think your ridiculous accusations will be listened to in the corridors of power? Trawden is hopelessly compromised and the scribblings of a drug addict will attract no more interest than the ramblings of a two year old. Which would leave you out on your own, the son of a known terrorist, making a series of unsubstantiated, preposterous claims. More whisky?"

Ellis was feeling slightly dizzy and declined. He felt like he was starting to draw out the real character of the man sitting before him. Most of his case was bluff, but Daid didn't know that. Despite all his training, all his experience, Daid couldn't stop himself showing his naked power when he had no real need.

"I tell you what we'll do, Mr Landsman. I'm prepared to overlook your allegations. You stay in this rural idyll, forget about the big city and we'll say no more about it. Of course I'll have to speak to Mr Trawden, but we've always been able to resolve our difficulties in the past. Are you feeling unwell Mr Landsman? You appear to have lost a little colour."

Ellis felt himself slumping in his chair. He wanted to tell this man about the mystery phone, about the information he'd been fed from somewhere inside the Brigade, about what Tom Cavanagh had told him. There was so much he wanted to say but his voice had disappeared. He tried to call out, hoping to attract Lorna's attention, but what emerged was little more than a squeak. It slowly dawned on him that his visitor must have drugged or poisoned him – something in the whisky no doubt.

He hoped his father would not choose this opportunity to make some final observations, well, maybe final on this side of the curtain. He struggled to hold on to consciousness but he could feel it ebbing away. The smiling face of his visitor began to recede slowly.

Daid collected the poisoned chalice, washed it and returned it to the table. He poured a small drop of whisky into the bottom of the glass. It looked better that way. He pocketed the whisky bottle, left the house and removed his latex gloves. It had stopped snowing, the moon was out. He breathed in deeply and walked across to his car.

Lorna heard the front door being closed and looked out of the bedroom window. She saw their visitor crossing the yard, approaching his car.

Lucas was hungry, starving even. Since he'd been hounded out of the pack, he'd struggled to survive. Time and again he'd returned to the house and found the scraps of food that had been left for him. But now he was desperate. He kept his eyes fixed on the man as he moved closer. He had to eat. He gathered what little of his strength remained, flexed his once powerful muscles and leapt from the bushes towards the man.

Lorna found it hard to work out what was happening. The man had been standing next to the 4x4, fumbling for his keys. There was a sudden movement behind him and he fell suddenly and heavily against the vehicle, striking his head on the wing mirror. He slumped to the ground.

She ran downstairs, shouting and then froze when she saw Ellis collapsed in the chair. Her shout turned into a scream. She couldn't tell at first whether he was still breathing, but he had a pulse. She found her phone and rang 999. They were reluctant to come out – it was the Outlands, it was snowing, they might get lost. Lorna was furious. She bellowed down the phone and threatened them with legal action. They said they'd try.

What more could she do? She hunted around for any clue as to what might have happened to Ellis. She could find no trace of a bullet or knife wound. As she glanced at the whisky glass, she wondered whether he could have been poisoned. She sat, drained and then suddenly recalled the scene she'd witnessed from the bedroom window. She was reluctant to leave Ellis but felt she needed to know whether there was still a threat of danger from outside.

She grabbed her coat and, casting a glance at Ellis, opened the front door. The car was still there. Of course it was – she'd heard no engine sound. She began to cross the yard. There was a shape lying on the ground next to the 4x4, and a smaller shape standing over it, teeth flashing in the moonlight, yellow eyes glinting. Lorna backed away, watching the wolf the whole time. It seemed like a good idea not to intervene.

She retreated and made her way across the rear yard to the bunkhouse. She heard the thump of the bassline. Toller wouldn't have heard her scream. There was no response to her hammering on the door, so she walked in. Toller was lying on the bed, eyes closed, oblivious to the world as the huge speakers blasted out a drum and bass track. He jumped a mile when she touched him on the shoulder. He was about to tear into her for invading his space, when he noticed her tears and ghostly pallor. He sat her down. She told him she'd called the ambulance, but was unsure about whether they'd turn up.

"No point in waiting for them bastards. They'll never bother. Do you drive?" She shook her head. "I'll take us in to Alexandria, to the hospital, though I'm not sure if that Land Rover will make it. Did you say there's another vehicle in the yard?" She nodded. "I'll go and check it out."

"Wait." She told him that the wolf was still there. He said he'd handle it.

Ellis had loaned him an old parka which was a couple of sizes too big and a pair of old boots. He put these on, stepped out into the snow and walked around the house to the front yard. He saw the body and the wolf. He found it hard to take in. He'd never seen a wolf before. He pulled his phone out of his pocket and took a picture of the macabre scene. He spoke in a low voice, trying to keep the wolf calm and at bay. He edged round to the driver's door and looked through the window. He was in luck. The keys were in the ignition. Still talking to the wolf, Toller opened the door as quietly as he could and climbed in.

The sound of the engine shattered the stillness of the night and the wolf backed off. Toller couldn't see exactly where the body was. He didn't want to drive over it, so he stepped out of the car, leaving the engine running. He edged around the vehicle. The body was slumped against the side of the car. He'd have to move it. The wolf watched as Toller pulled at the body, but it didn't budge. He tried again and slowly the dead weight shifted. He kept one eye on the creature, surprised that it hadn't attacked him.

Toller jumped back into the 4x4 and drove towards the house, pulling up outside the front door. He and Lorna managed to carry Ellis to the car, place him across the back seat and cover him with blankets. Lorna climbed into the passenger seat. Toller checked the fuel gauge. The tank was half full – his second piece of luck. He swung the vehicle round and the headlamp beam picked out the body in the snow, the wolf nearby.

"Wait. We can't leave him like that!" Lorna put her hand up to her mouth.

"Why not, after what he's done to your man? Anyway why should we deprive yon wolf of a feed?"

Lorna gripped the door handle and wiped her eyes. It was difficult to think. What should she do? How had all this happened? What had seemed almost like a game, had suddenly turned deadly serious.

"I…I just think it wouldn't be right. It doesn't feel decent somehow. I know he tried to kill Ellis but…".

"Look, er, Lorna, I'm not risking myself against old greybeard there. I know who the winner would be. And we don't know how much time we've got, I mean for Ellis."

Lorna said nothing. Toller took the opportunity of the silence and drove off down the track. He engaged the four wheel drive, avoided the brakes, drove on the gears. He managed to keep up a reasonable speed despite the conditions.

"Where did you learn to drive?" Lorna asked.

"Ah, we all drive, usually from about thirteen on something small and then move up to bigger vehicles when we get the chance. All nicked of course, no licences, no insurance, no MOTs. It's one way were not deprived." Toller looked across at Lorna and smiled. "Who's the man lying in the snow by the way?"

Lorna wondered how much to tell Toller.

"I'm not really sure. Ellis wasn't sure. He's from the Brigade, probably quite senior."

"Why was he talking to Ellis?"

"It was about the body Ellis found. He told you about it."

"So why would the Brig want to poison Ellis. It doesn't make sense… unless he'd found out something he shouldn't." Lorna didn't respond.

It took them an hour and a half to reach Alexandria. There was a small hospital on the outskirts but no A and E. Toller stayed in the car whilst Lorna went to the hospital reception. She explained that she thought Ellis had been poisoned, that she didn't know what the substance was. She was deliberately vague about the circumstances. The receptionist told her there was no way they could help, that she'd have to go into Glasgow. Near to tears, Lorna insisted that they had to help. Her raised voice attracted attention from one of the side wards. An Indian doctor came up to the desk.

"What seems to be the problem?" he asked and Lorna explained. "You may be in luck, Miss. I have some knowledge of poisons, one of my early specialities. Let's get the patient in here."

Ellis was loaded on to a trolley and wheeled in to an examination room. A nurse drew the curtain. Lorna sat outside on a red stacking chair drinking tepid tea from a plastic cup.

Toller sat nervously in the 4x4, wondering what the cameras might be picking up. He'd thought about the problem of the Tracka. Would anyone be monitoring the vehicle's movements? But even if they were, they'd assume it was the Brig man driving. And, maybe the Brig didn't have to use Trackas. He wound down the window to let out the cigarette smoke. How odd it was, the way things turned out – his mate dead, him living in the middle of nowhere, learning how to cut trees down. What would happen next? Would he do better just to take off somewhere, the 4x4 was a good drive, there was fuel in the tank? But he wouldn't get far. He was safer hiding out – at least for the time being.

The doctor returned and put a reassuring hand on Lorna's shoulder.

"I think he'll be OK. We'll need to keep him in for observation. I haven't been able to identify exactly what he's taken, but I've narrowed it down and I'll run some more detailed tests. What exactly happened?" The doctor rubbed the back of his hand across his forehead and took a sip of water from a bottle.

"That's the thing. I don't really know." Lorna played for time, not really sure what story to tell. "I know he'd been feeling down recently. He's had a lot of problems. Maybe it was all getting too much for him." It was safer not to mention anything to do with the Brig. The hospital would be obliged to report Ellis' arrival if they suspected any link to an investigation.

The doctor looked sympathetic. "Perhaps I shouldn't say this, but there's a lot of it about. We don't get it here so much, but talking to my city colleagues, it's rife. You're from the Outlands aren't you? That must be difficult. Are you going to stay in town until tomorrow?"

Lorna hadn't really thought about this. Where would she stay? What about Laska? What about the body? The doctor said there was a guest room at the hospital which wasn't occupied. She'd be welcome to use that. She thanked him and went out to talk to Toller.

He told her he'd go back to the house, feed the dog, get some sleep and come back in the morning to pick up her and hopefully Ellis as well.

"Do you want me to get rid of the corpse?" he added, in his usual blunt manner. She hadn't the slightest idea what to do. "I'll sort it," he said quickly.

She handed him the keys to the house and hoped she wouldn't regret it.

Toller found the journey back to Ellis' place easier than the trip out. He was enjoying himself, putting the Brazilia Roadster through its paces. There was no traffic. He couldn't believe how empty the landscape was. He thought he'd find it off-putting, scary even, but there was an attraction to it he'd not expected. His estate was so full of people. There was no escape. Most of the time he'd been OK with that, thrived on it in fact, but now and then he'd felt trapped, limited. He'd often thought he'd be lucky to get beyond twenty five. It'd be either the drugs, or the Brig or more likely one of the up and coming thugs – a thirteen year old probably. They were just complete headcases.

As he pulled into the yard at Ellis' house he realised he hadn't thought at all about what to do with the body. His comments to Lorna had been mainly bravado. He'd seen his fair share of corpses but someone else had always taken care of them.

The headlights picked out a mix of footprints in the snow. There was no sign of the wolf. He was grateful for that. They were OK in zoos but out here they should just be shot. He realised suddenly that there was no sign of the corpse either. Perhaps the snow had buried the body. He sniggered – wasn't that supposed to happen to bodies?

He stepped out of the vehicle and walked around kicking the snow in the area where he thought the body should be. There was nothing. He looked again at the footprints. Idiot – why hadn't he spotted it before? There were two sets of prints coming from the footpath to the loch and then returning. Someone else had been there and they'd obviously taken the body. There were traces of blood and an area where the snow had been flattened. This was all too weird. Who could have possibly known about the dead man? Would they be back? He retreated to his bunk house, locked and bolted the door, stoked the fire and lay on the floor fully dressed, under a blanket, next to the dog.

January 14th

Toller awoke with what felt like a hangover, except he hadn't been drinking. The pain in his head was nagging and persistent. He knew there was this big problem but it took him a while before he could give it some shape. A series of images flashed through his mind – the body in the snow, the wolf snarling, Ellis lying across the back seat of the car, Lorna trying to hold it together.

Still at least no one had descended on the house overnight, he hadn't been hauled away back to the city and when he checked outside, the 4x4 hadn't disappeared – unlike the body of the Brigman.

He found some eggs in the kitchen and made himself a sort of omelette. He was new to cooking, was slowly discovering what worked and what turned into an uneatable mess. As he drove off down the track, Laska sat up front, keen to keep an eye on their progress. The few vehicles they passed were on farming business, over-sized tractors towing even bigger trailers. The journey to the hospital seemed quicker than it had the previous evening. He wondered what would await him. He hoped Ellis had pulled through.

Toller stayed in the vehicle when he reached the hospital car park. He didn't want to be picked up by the hospital's cameras. He sat hoping that Lorna would come out at some stage to check whether he'd arrived. Laska seemed uneasy, perhaps sensing that Ellis was nearby. After about half an hour Toller saw Lorna come out of the hospital's front door and stand there taking deep breaths. When she spotted the 4x4, she walked over to greet Toller and the dog.

"How's your man?" he asked cautiously.

"Awake thank God," Lorna said. She looked exhausted.

"Did they find out what the stuff was?"

"They're still doing more tests but they're pretty confident from all the tests so far that he'll be OK. But he's going to find eating difficult for a while – the poison affected his gut. Do you want to come in and see him?"

Toller shook his head and explained why.

"That's fair enough," Lorna said. "We can take him home soon, all being well. Is there something else bothering you Toller?"

"Aye. It's the body."

"Oh Jesus! How could I have forgotten? What did you do with it?"

"Nothing. It wasn't there. Someone's moved it."

Lorna wasn't sure if she could cope with all this.

She went back into the hospital. There were some forms to fill in. She lied where necessary, trying to keep their story as simple as possible. It helped that the hospital had a record of a previous admission involving Ellis, when he'd had a minor argument with a chainsaw. That established him as a bona fide Outland resident, rather than someone on the run.

Lorna breathed a huge sigh of relief once the 4x4 pulled off the hospital car park and headed north. Ellis lay on the back seat. He was trying to reconstruct what had happened the previous night, but kept losing the thread, his mind floating off anywhere but where he wanted it to be.

When they reached Kintrawe House, Ellis settled on the sofa and dozed. Toller retreated to the bunk house to catch up on his sleep. Lorna remembered the mystery phone which, in all the

drama of the previous evening, they'd left behind. She was relieved
– there was no new message. Ellis suddenly sat up.

"I need to speak to Gam. He'll have to come here. We need to
retaliate. Can you call him?"

Lorna nodded, but she was worried about Ellis. He was in no
fit state to talk sensibly about anything, let alone how to strike back
against the Brigade.

+ + +

Daid lay still in the small bed. He was sweating badly, his throat
was parched and the pain in his arm was excruciating. It was
strange to think that it was his lighter that had saved him. He
closed his eyes for a moment. He saw the tail lights of his 4x4
disappearing down the track and the wolf moving towards him
menacingly, his jaws open. Daid could see the wound on his arm,
deep and raw, the blood gradually congealing in the cold night air.
The pain was dulled. He cursed the wolf as it got nearer and
nearer, drawn to the exposed flesh. It took an enormous effort for
Daid to use his good arm to repeatedly spark up his lighter inches
from the wolf's face. Then he called Trawden.

Daid opened his eyes. He was back in the small bed. McPhee
had told him about the rescue, the boat journey and Trawden's
tame doctor who'd patched him up and given him a shot of
morphine.

He was feeling dreadful. The pain in his arm was getting
worse, his whole body was aching, he shivered constantly and his
head was splitting. He wanted just to sleep, but he knew that, first,
he had to call Cormack.

"So, did it work?" Cormack sounded distant, almost
disinterested.

"Well he was on his way out when I left him, but I don't know for certain. Listen I'm going to be laid up for a couple of days. I'm feeling dreadful. This bloody wolf attacked me, took a huge chunk out of my arm."

Cormack interrupted him. "Did you say a wolf?"

"Yes a wolf. Why don't you listen! Look I need rest. You'll have to cover for me in the meantime and find out what's happened to Landsman. If he's still alive, he'll have guessed what happened. He won't be able to prove anything, but all the same he could be dangerous. Use your imagination as to the best way to deal with him."

+ + +

Cormack wrote a few lines in his notebook. That feeling of smugness was there again. A key piece of the jigsaw was now in place. He phoned Brigadier Cutting at the Pyramid and updated him, telling him as much as he needed to know.

He enjoyed the walk to his sister's apartment. He found himself whistling as he walked. Aran was pleased to see him.

"So did you enjoy your meet-up with Carla then?" he asked, trying not to smirk. His sister's look showed him that she obviously did. "Good. I've come to tell you that after a visit to talk to Mr Landsman, our leader is currently indisposed." Aran looked interested. "Yes, as you know, I've been worried about him for a while. Those problems I mentioned to you have caught up with him at last. He managed to identify the main source of his difficulties and asked me to help him deal with it. But he's ended up as the biter bit. I blame myself in a way. Maybe the merchandise I helped him get hold of was not as effective as it should have been."

"Iain – you look like you never intended the merchandise – whatever it was – to be effective. What have you been up to?"

"I've no idea what you mean, Aran."

She'd watched his career progress over the years, pleased but surprised that he'd risen so quickly. Maybe it wouldn't be long before there was another move upwards.

"So, with Mr Pelham departed and now Mr Daid indisposed, what happens next?"

"Who knows," her brother replied, "but maybe it's the end of the old dinosaur era. We'll have to wait and see."

"And what will happen to Mr Landsman now?"

"Well we can't leave a dangerous man like that roaming free, can we? We'll have to bring him in."

January 7th

Ferguson House was an anonymous 1980's block, on the north side of the city, just beyond the M8. It had been mothballed for years during the depression, but had recently had a minor makeover.

Lemmy waited in the sparsely furnished reception area, sipping from a water bottle. There was nobody around. After ten minutes a clerk wandered in to the room and took his place behind the desk. He was dressed like a pall bearer. Lemmy explained who he'd come to see, using the name Cormack had mentioned and was given a pass and instructed to go in the lift to room 614.

As the lift creaked its way upwards Lemmy rehearsed what he was going to say. He seldom felt nervous, but this meeting was different. Cormack hadn't sounded too happy on the phone. But as he was very much the control freak, he wouldn't like the fact that there was a problem. The lift halted and the doors opened. He stepped out into a long corridor, cheap carpet on the floor, cheap Impressionist prints on the walls. Room 614 was furthest from the lift. Through a long narrow window at the end of the corridor Lemmy could see a construction site – a new bank building was slowly creeping skywards. He knocked on the door and walked in.

He was surprised to see that Cormack was his usual cool self, no hint of annoyance.

"Sit down Charlesworth. What's so important that you couldn't tell me on the phone?" Cormack poured coffee from a jug into two mugs. "We've got thirty minutes."

"Thank you for seeing me. What I've got to say is a little sensitive, so telling you over the phone didn't seem appropriate. I'll come straight to the point. I've reason to believe that some of the freelancing work is out of control. By that I mean the disappearances and the terminations." Cormack didn't react. "As far as I can tell, these activities are officially sanctioned. I thought you should know." He handed his boss a folder which detailed some of the more extreme activities.

Cormack flicked through it in a cursory manner and placed the file on a small glass-topped table.

"And how did you come across this highly sensitive information?"

Lemmy had to stop himself smiling. He didn't want to appear facetious.

"Well, I am an agent, I've worked undercover for years as you know and it's my job to dig around and find the dirt – wherever it might be."

"So, what do you want me to do about this?" Cormack asked.

Lemmy thought he sounded pre-occupied. He decided he might as well take the bull by the horns.

"Well I'm assuming that these activities haven't been given the green light at the top of the organisation. So, firstly they should be stopped and secondly there should be some sort of internal enquiry – short and sweet. I can see we wouldn't want to broadcast publicly what's been happening. I know it's a sensitive area, but that cuts both ways, particularly if it continues unchecked and subsequently leaks out."

"I never took you to be the sensitive type, Charlesworth." Cormack's tone was withering. "After all you're a man who's done time, if memory serves me right. As it happens, I anticipated that this might be your concern and I've carried out a little research of my own. In all recent cases where there's been a fatality, there has been a clear self-defence justification. There will of course be J1 enquiries for these cases, but I have every confidence that the agents concerned will be vindicated in their actions. As for the so-called disappearances, we have an off-shore holding facility for some of our more troublesome clients. Under Section 17 of the Security Act we are entitled to delay informing relatives of such detentions for a period of up to three months. And of course these periods can be extended, where such a course of action is warranted. I'm surprised that an agent of your experience was not aware of these facts. You will now return to your approved duties and leave any consideration of wider issues to your superiors. If you were to raise these concerns again, in any forum, you would be subject to immediate dismissal. After all your years of service that would be a shame. Is that clear?"

Lemmy rapidly revised his view of Cormack. He'd initially sensed something a little different about the man, a slight unorthodoxy perhaps. He realised he'd been sadly mistaken.

"That's very clear, sir," he said. He left the room in silence.

Cormack picked up the file and placed it in his briefcase. He'd come down hard on Charlesworth because he didn't want him digging any deeper. He'd provided sufficient ammunition already. In reality, Cormack wasn't at all sure what the outcome of any one of the J1 enquiries would be. As he walked to his car, his phone rang. It was Garside his assistant.

"Bad news I'm afraid, sir. I've just had a call from our friend Mr Trawden. It appears that the Commander has passed away. Complications apparently from the dog bite. It must have had rabies or something similar. The doctor never spotted it."

"OK Garside. Have you spoken to anyone else about this?"

"No sir."

"Good, because what we're going to do is pin this attack on Landsman's dog – you remember, the one you drugged. That way we'll have something else to use to get at Landsman. Is that clear?"

"Perfectly sir."

Cormack sat in the silence of the car. He was smiling. So the wolf had got his man. It was a fitting end for Daid. But the opportunity to name the dog as the attacker and blame Landsman was too good to miss. It was one more nail he'd be able to use to hammer into the backwoodsman's coffin. He was thinking figuratively of course.

He didn't want Landsman running around any longer. He'd served his purpose.

* January 8th

I suppose I've been dreading something like this happening. Just after I started at Spook Central, I made a flippant comment to Morrisey about the boys doing the exciting agent stuff and the girls stuck inside over their machines. Well it's come back to haunt me.

I had my regular meeting with C yesterday and he dropped a real bombshell. He sat there and told me that Daid was dead. I had to stop myself breathing a sigh of relief. C himself looked untroubled. Maybe they didn't get on. I tried to compose myself and take in the detail of my instructions. My task is to apprehend Ellis Landsman, the man responsible for Daid's death. He lives in the Outlands and my job is to interview him and then bring him in. I don't know why he hasn't been apprehended already. There's obviously something sensitive going on. Should I be pleased that I've been entrusted with this task? I'm not sure what they'll do with Landsman – but I fear the worst. In my book he's a hero. I certainly won't lose any sleep over the Commander's death.

I met up with Aran for the first time yesterday evening. I'd looked forward to it for so long, but I have to say it was a bit of a let down. Something about her has changed. She's not exactly distant, but she's not the kind of lover she used to be. It's hard to be specific. I told her about my worries about Landsman but she was really unsympathetic. She said it was an order and I should just get on with it and let others worry about the consequences. She's got a point. I tried to phone Lemmy but it just went through to voicemail.

So here I am, parked in a lay-by on the road up north, eating a sandwich and wondering what Landsman's going to be like. Before I bring him in, I've got to interview him about his involvement in the Commander's death so that I can then brief the interrogating officer out at Mount Florida. It'll be strange to go back there. C told me that Landsman might be a little reluctant to come in (surprise, surprise). So the second part of my approach is to talk to him about a Sergeant Lambert, who's apparently a friend of his. He's under interrogation about leaking classified information to Landsman and has asked his friend to be called as a witness. C reckons that Landsman won't refuse, because of the closeness of their friendship. It seems a bit odd to me. You don't normally get the chance to call an external witness for an internal hearing, let alone have him chauffeured in. Still that's the order.

Must remember I'm Hammerton not Lucini. You'd think it would be second nature by now. I don't want any slip ups. Time to go.

January 8th

Gam had been reluctant to make the journey out to Kintrawe House, but he felt he owed it to Ellis to show up. Lorna had told him about the poisoning and painted a bleak picture. His van had only just managed to complete the journey. He'd had to stop three times to make minor repairs. And he'd forgotten to fit the simulator to the Tracka, until he'd gone a good thirty miles.

When he arrived and saw Ellis, he was shocked. His moments of clarity seemed all too fleeting. They talked about how best to use Ellis' story. Gam played for time. He felt that running any kind of story involving the top Brigade officer would be playing with fire. The Brig had already been stepping up their campaign of harassment against him and any story involving the Commander would surely seal his fate.

Lorna sensed Gam's reluctance, but Ellis didn't seem to notice it. The mystery mobile reverberated. She checked the message.

"It's another text, Ellis." She'd been trying her best to keep things together ever since their return from the hospital. A voice in her head kept telling her to bail out, but she continued to ignore it.

"What does it say?" Ellis was suddenly animated.

"There's a woman from the Brigade coming to see you. She should be here in an hour or so. There's no other detail."

"They must know about Daid. Perhaps they're coming to finish me off, give me a drop more so to speak. Good job I've got an insurance policy isn't it?"

"What do you mean?" Lorna's voice was shaking. "And don't joke about what they might do to you."

"You'll find out soon enough. I'd almost forgotten about it in all the excitement. Better make sure Toller is out of the way when our visitor arrives. It wouldn't be good for any of us if he was discovered here. Are you OK, Gam?" Gam had suddenly gone very pale, risen from his seat and started pacing the room.

"I can't let the Brig catch me here, not with my track record. I'll have to leave."

"It's no problem, Gam. Put your van round the back in one of the sheds. There's an old tarpaulin you can use to cover it up. Stay out of the way in the bunk house with Toller. You'll be perfectly safe. I can't see her doing a search."

Gam followed his instructions without another word. Ellis told Lorna that he had a couple of things to do on the laptop before their guest arrived.

Ellis was no technical genius. He fiddled around with the laptop, plugging in and un-plugging various leads. He was still finding movement quite draining and stopped frequently, sweating and shaking. He wiped his forehead with tissues and took long drinks of water. At last he was satisfied with his handiwork. He copied the results on to a disc. He kept on wanting to lie down and sleep, but managed to resist the temptation. He had another sudden question for Lorna.

"That 4x4 – the one Daid came in. What happened to it? We don't want this Brigade woman tripping over it."

"Oh yes – I meant to tell you. Toller took it into Alexandria and swapped it for another model, one that didn't have the disadvantage of being owned by the Brig."

"What do you mean 'swapped'?"

"Apparently he has a cousin on one of the estates in the town and they arranged a deal. The vehicle Toller's got in exchange isn't quite the same spec, but then it's not hot – well as far as we know anyway."

Ellis and Lorna sat waiting on the sofa. Neither of them could summon up the energy to do anything else. When they heard the sound of an approaching vehicle, they looked towards the window. The snow was in temporary remission and they heard the tyres of the vehicle scrunching over the gravel at the end of the track.

Lorna gave Ellis a hug. He hauled himself from the sofa, opened the front door and stepped outside. The car was a small high-powered convertible. He didn't recognise the make. He thought there was something very attractive about the woman who was easing herself out of the driver's seat. Her loose limbs seemed to move effortlessly. She walked across the yard and held her hand out. He shook it. This wasn't at all what he'd expected.

"Sorry to arrive like this, with such short notice. My name's Hammerton. I'm from the Brigade and I need to talk to you about Commander Daid, but also about your friend Sergeant Lambert. He's in trouble. Is it OK for me to come in?"

"Yes, certainly." Ellis found his usual defences were down. Who was this woman? He was expecting to be questioned about Daid, but was taken aback by the reference to Ross. What had happened to him?

Carla was somewhat surprised when she saw Lorna in the sitting room. Nobody had informed her that Landsman had a partner. Perhaps they were unaware. She noticed the dog dozing on the hearthrug and had difficulty reconciling this image with the attack dog that Cormack had described.

"Now, this is all a little awkward. You see Mr Daid, who visited you here very recently, has unfortunately passed away."

Lorna looked at Ellis. They both tried not to show any emotion or surprise.

"And you were one of the last people to see him alive, Mr

Landsman. I understand that he was attacked by your dog at…"
she hesitated, "… your instigation. His death arose because of
complications arising from that attack." She paused to allow this
information to sink in. "Control of the dog is obviously your
responsibility and I'm afraid I'll need to take you in for questioning,
Mr Landsman." To her surprise, Landsman burst out laughing.

"You people are priceless, Miss…er… Hammerton. Your
Commander paid me a visit. That part of your comments is
accurate. I don't know who told you the fairy story about Laska
here." Ellis pointed to the sleeping dog. "Now, what you may not
know is that your Commander was involved in the death of
someone called Rebecca Leuchars and he was also responsible for
attempting to murder me."

Carla was completely taken aback. The short briefing she'd
been given by Cormack had clearly been completely inadequate –
unless of course he was unaware of these claims.

"These are very serious accusations, Mr Landsman. Why have
you not made a formal report to the Brigade? Could it be that you
have no actual evidence?"

Ellis rose suddenly from his chair and Carla was briefly
worried for her own safety. But her host moved to the table and
opened a laptop. She noticed that his movements were shaky and
poorly co-ordinated.

"Come and have a look, Miss Hammerton. I think you may
be interested."

The three of them gathered around the screen and Ellis
pressed a key to play a video. It wasn't good quality but they could
definitely hear Ellis' tinny voice coming out of the laptop speakers.
He turned the sound up. The film was grainy but two figures were
visible. The man who wasn't Ellis was tall, well built. He was
talking about Rebecca. The film showed Ellis leaving the room
and then the other man poured something into Ellis' drink.

"Look at the bastard! That's the poison, going into your drink – look, there!" Lorna could hardly contain herself. The man was attempting to kill Ellis and they'd got it on tape. It was only luck that he hadn't died.

The film continued and showed Ellis eventually slumping in his seat, Daid tidying up and then leaving the room. Lorna held on to Ellis' arm. The film ended and he turned to their visitor and inclined his head.

"Doesn't reflect well on the Brigade does it? A lot of people suspect them of foul play but it's another thing to have irrefutable evidence of it in black and white, with the top man in the lead role."

Lorna stared at Ellis trying to take in what she'd just witnessed. She had a sudden thought and fumbled in her bag for her phone. She flicked through a series of pictures until she found the one she wanted and showed it to Hammerton. The scene was starkly lit by the camera flash, a man spread-eagled on the ground, a deep gash in his right arm, blood oozing from the wound and standing over him a wolf poised to attack again. Ellis looked at the picture over the officer's shoulder. He looked as astonished as Carla. He was about to ask Lorna who'd taken the picture but stopped himself just in time.

"So, in case you've been wondering, the photo should establish the dog's innocence," Lorna said, failing to keep the venom out of her voice.

Carla's head was spinning, her case falling apart in front of her. She did her utmost to keep a measured tone.

"I have to admit that this evidence raises some serious questions which I cannot answer. And of course the Commander is not able to mount any kind of defence."

Ellis thought the Brigade woman was finding it hard going, as if she was trying to decide which way to jump. She asked Lorna for a glass of water. Lorna fetched a jug of water and three glasses. The agent took a long drink. "That's amazing water, far better than we have in the city."

"It's straight from the burn," Ellis said.

"Can I be frank with you?" The drink seemed to have revived her. "I have to take you back to Glasgow Mr Landsman. Sergeant Lambert is accused of supplying classified information to you which has compromised security. The consequences are probably more serious for him than they are for you. I trust you will want to attend to assist your friend. With regard to the death of the Commander I shall report what you have told me. I'll need a copy of the photograph that's on your phone. This is my number" she said looking at Lorna. "But as to the film, as you'll realise, it's dynamite. My advice would be to say nothing of this to the Brigade – or anyone else. Without being too dramatic, your life might be in danger if this were to become public. Of course I shouldn't be saying this and I'll deny any knowledge of the film if you should raise it."

Ellis couldn't believe what he'd just heard. Was this the Brigade talking? Again he wondered who the woman really was and what her underlying motives were. He decided to take a gamble.

"Does the name Darkstone mean anything to you?"

She was good. Just a slight spasm gave her away. "I'm afraid not, Mr Landsman. What is it?"

"An underground dirty tricks project in Glasgow, controlled by SecureUK from their London HQ."

"Why are you making such outlandish claims and where did you get this information from?"

"A man called Lemmy told me." Again, he noticed her response was almost completely controlled – almost but not quite.

"I have to say you don't sound very convincing. Is there a point to this?"

"Not really, I just wanted to see what your reaction would be."

Ellis looked directly at her. She looked away unable to keep her composure. Lorna thought it might be the after-effects of the poisoning that were still effecting Ellis' judgement. Why else would he be giving yet more incriminating and unsolicited information to a Brigade officer?

"Given the forecast, I really think we need to go, Mr Landsman. Do you have a toilet I can use?" Lorna showed her the way and returned to the living room.

"How on earth did you get that footage?" Lorna looked intrigued and worried in equal measure.

"I bought the camera after the break-in and the attack on Laska. The camera's tiny – it's up there over the fireplace. But I'd never got round to activating it. But when Daid was on his way I suddenly thought about using it and I'm damned glad I did."

"But aren't you worried about having the footage?"

"Of course, but it's going to be a very useful lever – maybe not right now, but in the near future. Did you see her face when Daid was up to his poisoning tricks? I still can't fathom why he didn't use a sufficient dose. I mean aren't they supposed to be professionals at that kind of thing?"

"Don't joke about it love. Don't forget it so very nearly worked." Lorna curled up against Ellis and stroked the back of his head. "I don't think you should go – you're still not well."

"I haven't got any choice. She may be polite, but underneath she's still a Brigade officer. And if I can help Ross at all…well I think I owe him one. I'm going to ask Toller to tail us. It may be useful to have him nearby, you know, if things get difficult."

Carla returned to the room. Ellis stood a little too suddenly and had to hold on to the mantelpiece for support.

"I just need to check the sheep before we go. They're in a pen at the back of the house. I'll be a few minutes. Is that OK?" She told him that would be fine.

Ellis went out by the back door and walked down to the sheep pen. Toller was there clearing out the bottom end of the shed, to create space for the lambs.

"Are you up for following someone from the Brig?"

"No problem. What's the score?"

Ellis explained as quickly as he could, said he should keep a good distance until they reached the built up areas. Toller's Mumbai Delta was a dull grey so wouldn't be particularly noticeable.

"When we get there – wherever there is – can you wait for me? If I don't show within two hours, I want you to phone Lorna and tell her and then phone this number. You can trust this guy if he asks you to do something to help. You alright with that?"

"Sure thing, boss." Toller had taken to calling Ellis boss, always with a smirk. The two of them got on well enough despite or maybe because they had very little in common.

Ellis told him to sneak a look at the woman's car before they set off, so he'd know what he'd be following. Gam was standing in the woodshed looking uncomfortable. Ellis asked him if he'd take Lorna and Laska back to Glasgow with him.

"Tell her to take the laptop, the disc and her phone of course." Gam nodded. Ellis phoned Eric, his neighbour and asked him if he'd feed and keep an eye on the livestock, in his absence.

Ellis returned to the house. He got the impression that Hammerton was about to say something, but she remained silent. He kissed Lorna and whispered something in her ear, then followed the agent to her car. As the vehicle set off down the drive, Lorna heard Toller's vehicle starting up at the back of the house. He waved as he passed and she saw his brake lights at the bend. Even though Gam was there, she felt suddenly very alone.

Toller kept his distance from the Mini Cooper S up ahead. Turnings off the road were few and far between so it made the job

relatively simple. For once he drove without music playing. He
didn't want any reverberating basslines to be heard by the car
ahead. He thought about how things were turning out. The
nightmares about Dommo were getting less frequent. He was
felling trees on a regular basis and was learning about the messy
business of lambing. The food was decent enough and the
homemade booze was plentiful. The dog was great company. It
was the lasses he missed, inevitably. A few times he'd sneaked off
to Alexandria and ended up having fumbled sex on the back seat
of a car. Usually he didn't even know their names, but his cousin
seemed to know them all.

It had taken him a while to work out what was going on. He'd
picked up part of the story from Ellis when they'd been out felling.
Lorna seemed a lot more approachable than she had been and now
and then she'd confide in him about her concerns. The clincher
though was when, earlier, he'd hung around in the kitchen,
eavesdropping on the conversation between the Brig woman and
Ellis in the living room. That gave him a complete picture. He just
wished he could have seen the camera footage.

As the road widened and buildings became more frequent, the
traffic increased and he moved a little closer to the bright blue
sports car. He had some difficulty keeping track of it going
through the centre of Glasgow, but traffic eased as they drove on
to Mount Florida. The Mini halted in front of a four-storey
concrete office block. From a distance, Toller saw the two
occupants get out of the car and enter the building. He looked at
his watch and slumped low in the seat. He could see the entrance
to the office block through his wing mirror. Two hours max he
thought as he lit up.

To Ellis' surprise, the lift went down four floors. He looked at
Hammerton's reflection in the mirror on the back wall of the lift,
hoping not to make it too obvious. He tried to work out what it

was about her that was so attractive. They waited briefly in the foyer area and were then ushered into a brightly lit room.

Ross Lambert was seated at the far end of the table. They exchanged furtive glances. Ellis was placed at the opposite end of the table from his friend. Hammerton spoke out of earshot to a small man with a thin, mean face. The man started speaking.

"I'm Sergeant Major Garside." He sat in an over-sized leather chair, his pen poised above a small notebook. He scribbled a few lines before looking up.

Ellis suddenly remembered Ross telling him that he thought Garside had been the one who'd broken into his house and attacked Laska. He tried to put the thought out of his mind. He needed to concentrate. A clerk who was sitting next to Garside stood up, took a sheet of paper and read out the charge. It was almost comically formal.

"The Strathclyde Brigade submits that Sergeant Ross Lambert supplied classified information to Mr Ellis Landsman, a civilian, contrary to sub section 3 of section 27 of the Information Control Act. The Brigade further submits that Mr Landsman colluded in this process in the knowledge that the information he requested was classified."

Ellis realised he should have expected the charge. Had Hammerton's approach caused him to lower his defences? He wondered what the charade of a trial was really all about.

Garside started the interrogation. It was low-key, no threats or shouting. Ellis realised Hammerton wasn't involved in the hearing and she looked uncomfortable, as if she didn't really want to be there. Ross seemed to be going through the motions. He looked a beaten man, completely subdued. Ellis wasn't given a chance to speak, other than to answer a few simple questions. Garside finished writing and announced that he found both defendants guilty. He stated that Sergeant Lambert would be detained in the building for further interrogation on related matters.

"Mr Landsman, you will be taken to Brigade Headquarters for questioning regarding additional serious charges."

Ellis had begun to suspect that the proceedings were just a preliminary to the more serious business. He wondered whether to say anything about his film, about how Daid really had met his death, but decided to keep silent for the time being.

Garside told him that he'd have to be cuffed for the journey to HQ. When Ellis objected, he was told it was standard procedure. The plastic ties cut into his wrists. He was led out to a waiting car, large, black, with tinted windows. The driver didn't speak. Ellis wondered where Toller was.

As they drove off, a vehicle reversed at high speed out of a parking bay and rammed into the driver's door. Ellis tried to open his door but, because of the cuffs, couldn't reach the handle. Suddenly the door flew open and Toller hauled him out and led him to the Delta. He floored the accelerator and shot off towards the dual carriageway. He lit a cigarette and hit a preset on his phone, the steering wheel wedged between his knees.

"Malky – listen, I need to swap my wheels right now. Am on the Florida dual, just by the water tower, heading east, you know? Good man. See you in the lay-by, after the burger place. Just dump this one in the quarry. It's nice enough but a wee bit hot." He finished the call and slowed down slightly. "As soon as I saw you with the cuffs on, I knew you'd need a hand."

"I don't know what to say."

"Don't say nothing. You rescued me pal. Now it's my turn."

He swerved off the road, into a lay-by and manoeuvred the car into a space between two piles of grit covered by tarpaulins. Toller pulled a multi-tool from his pocket, cut off the plastic ties and offered Ellis a smoke. The two of them sat there puffing nervously. It was only two or three minutes, but it seemed a lot longer. A small green car, a Ford, Ellis thought, pulled into the lay-by and two scrawny youths leapt out. They high-fived Toller, nodded to Ellis, pulled him out of the car, jumped in the Delta and sped off. Toller stubbed his cigarette out and they got into the Ford. He drove off at a normal speed, the radio playing softly.

"So, I've been thinking," Toller said. "The plan is we head over to Bathgate, to my uncle's place. Well he's not really my uncle. He's a mate of my brother's. He'll put us up for a couple of days until you can sort something else out. That's if you don't mind slumming it. That OK with you?"

"Thanks Toller, that sounds great," was all Ellis could manage. He fell asleep, exhausted by the events of the day. Toller wished the dog was with them.

* January 9th

Lambert seems a decent sort of guy. I wonder why they're really after him – probably because he's too decent. It's a weakness in this job. I can't make my mind up about Landsman. On the plus side it was indirectly down to him that Daid snuffed it. And he was the one who worked out what had happened to Leuchars. He may be an amateur but he's got some grit.

But then there's what Garside told me after that joke of an interrogation. He said that Landsman had told my mother I was dead. How could he have done such a thing? You'd think he'd have done some double checking before spreading news of my death far and wide. I must see them – mother and father. But I don't know how to do it. I can't just ring mother up, or walk in unannounced. I'll have to get someone else to break the news to them first. But who? It can't be Aran obviously. Maybe Lemmy would, if I could only contact him. Still no reply from him. What's he up to?

The other surprise about Landsman was his escape. I didn't think he had it in him. I was told that some kid had rammed the car he was in and spirited him away.

I was still down in the Mount Florida dungeon when it all kicked off, so I knew nothing about the escape until later. I found out C was in the building, so I asked to see him. I reckoned in the end I couldn't keep the information about Landsman's film to myself, so I spoke to C about it. I said I thought we had incredibly limited grounds for pursuing him further. Receipt of classified information maybe, but

*that's hardly a hanging offence. C just sat there looking inscrutable
when I told him. Sometimes it's impossible to guess what he's
thinking. Then he told me to go and find Landsman and bring him
in – just like that.*

*But C had at least taken in what I'd just told him. I was to
inform Landsman that he'd be coming in by agreement, that he
wouldn't be under arrest and that the slate would be wiped clean –
with no outstanding charges. I was to tell him that they'd even drop
the charges against Sergeant Lambert. Although he didn't show any
concern, C must be really worried about how Landsman might use
both the film and the dirt he's got about Daid's criminal activities.*

*But, how do I find the man? He's on the run. He could be
anywhere. I must speak to Lemmy.*

January 9ᵗʰ

Toller's 'uncle' ran a car repair garage and lived in the flat above. He was a man of few words and just grunted his approval when Toller had asked him if it was OK to stay. There was a spare room with bunk beds and no other furniture. Ellis slept long into the morning. When he woke, Toller brought him a bacon sandwich and a mug of tea from the take-away across the road. Toller told him he'd had a call from Lorna and he'd put her in the picture. She was worried sick and Gam was no better.

"She said I should mention the name 'Lemmy' to you, if that means anything."

"Yes it does, thanks. He may be able to help. Um, would it be OK to use your phone? Mine's bound to be tapped."

Toller handed him his mobile. Ellis tried to remember Lemmy's number. He'd learnt to avoid writing down this kind of information. It wouldn't come to him. He sipped the tea and devoured the sandwich. He realised that he'd eaten very little in the previous twenty-four hours. He leafed through the local free paper that had been left on the floor and flicked from car crashes, to break-ins, to fund-raising events for the local hospital. He wondered if it would be OK to phone Lorna. Maybe they'd be tapping her phone by now. He decided to risk it.

Lorna was delighted to hear from him and had to keep her emotions in check. She told him Laska had settled into her flat and that she was trying to persuade their friend to start writing. He knew immediately she was referring to Gam.

Ellis told her he loved her. Afterwards he realised he'd never said that to a woman before, not even Tora. He'd always held back.

He suddenly remembered he'd given Lemmy's number to Toller the previous day.

"Do you have that phone number I gave you yesterday?" he asked.

Toller pulled the scrap of paper from his pocket. Ellis' call went to voicemail. He wasn't sure what to say and in the end said nothing. He finished the call and sat for a while listening to the roar of a motorbike engine being tested in the garage below. He couldn't concentrate. Ever since the poisoning, he'd had problems trying to think straight. He worried that it might have done him some permanent damage. His phone rang.

"Ellis, what you up to?" It was Lemmy's reassuring voice.

Ellis explained, as briefly as he could, what had happened, trying to avoid anything that might sound too incriminating to an eavesdropper.

"OK I've got the gist of it. Can you get to Edinburgh?"

Ellis said he could.

"Good. I'll see you at a bar. It's the same name as the street where you and I met that first time – you remember?"

"But we haven't met in Edinburgh before." Ellis felt his mind fogging up again.

"No, no, I mean the first time, at the seaside, the name of the street there."

Ellis suddenly had a picture of it in his mind – the red pantiles, the sea front, what was the name of it? Think man, think. 'The Parade', that was it.

"Yes, I've got it now. When?"

"Today, 4:00 pm OK?"

Ellis agreed and breathed a sigh of relief. He didn't feel he could stay much longer in the garage flat. His head was buzzing. He finished his tea. He went to look for Toller and found him in the workshop under an old Jaguar. He was impressed by Toller's flexibility and his constant ability to adapt to new surroundings.

"Beautiful motor," Toller said when he saw Ellis peering under the vehicle. "This is what you call a car. You OK, big man?"

Ellis explained he needed another favour.

"No problem, we'll take this one for a spin, once I put some plates on."

Toller headed for the motorway. Ellis relaxed back into the worn leather seats and promptly fell asleep. Toller wound his window down and let the cold wind blow through his hair. He was more and more confident about not being caught. He had relatives in the capital. He'd call in on them, maybe stock up on some weed. He knew 'The Parade'. It was a large, chain pub, just off the Grassmarket. The M8 was busy but not choked. He made good progress and pulled off onto the A71 for the last part of the journey. He roused Ellis and dropped him off just above the Grassmarket..

"You sure you'll be OK? Do you want me to come along, I can always park up."

Ellis' first instinct was to say no. He didn't want to drag the lad any deeper into his problems. Then he changed his mind. He was definitely only functioning on half a brain and felt vulnerable, like he needed a minder.

"That would be great, if you don't mind."

Toller found space to park in a back yard off Cowgate. He spoke to a man in overalls and handed him a tenner.

"Space and security – can't be bad," he said as they headed off to 'The Parade'.

The front of the bar was heaving and raucous. Most of the drinkers were watching a boxing match on the big screen. Ellis was relieved to find Lemmy already ensconced in a corner at the rear of the bar. The two men hugged and Ellis introduced Toller. Lemmy gave him a twenty to get a round in.

"Is he OK?" Lemmy asked. "I mean can we trust him? Sounds like some pretty sensitive stuff you're about to tell me."

Ellis explained briefly what Toller had done for him already.

"Fair enough! I just don't want to make things more difficult than they already are."

Toller returned with two pints of proper beer as he called it and a pint of lager for himself. He'd also bought a pie and gravy and handed it across to Ellis.

"Thought you might be needing this, with you being so hungry and all."

Ellis nodded his thanks and picked up the knife and fork. Half way through his first mouthful he spluttered and coughed.

"Is the pie not OK?" Toller asked.

Ellis looked across the bar to check he hadn't been hallucinating. Coming towards him was the woman from Mount Florida, what was her name again, Hammerton? How could she have followed him here? Had someone been feeding her information?

"What's Hammerton doing here? Is this some sort of set up Lemmy?"

Toller immediately looked concerned. His hand went to his pocket, but Lemmy immediately calmed things down. He smiled, leaned across to Ellis and whispered "You're right, this is Janette Hammerton, but her real name is Carla Lucini."

Ellis clearly couldn't take it in. Toller read the body language and relaxed his grip on his pocket knife.

"You'll be wanting a drink, Miss. What'll it be?"

"Same as yours," she replied glancing at Toller's lager. He picked up some of Lemmy's change that was sitting in a pool of spilt beer on the table and wandered off to the bar again.

Ellis couldn't cope with the news. He sat staring at Carla Lucini unable to believe it.

"But how can it be Carla? Why is she here?"

"I appreciate it must be something of a shock for you. We can't say too much, but Carla and I have been working together on Darkstone." Lemmy whispered the word. Ellis nodded. "She phoned to tell me what had happened to you up at Mount Florida and about your Great Escape. When I got your call, I told Carla to come over so we could all meet up. All three of us are after the same thing in different ways. You'll just have to take my word for that."

Ellis took his time to let all this new information sink in. Then he suddenly remembered about Carla's parents. He began to shake and wasn't sure he could handle the situation.

"What is it Ellis? Are you OK?" Lemmy put an arm around his shoulder. Ellis took his time before replying.

"Look, I don't know how to say this, Carla, but when I was told it was your body I'd found in my wood, I went to visit your parents to give then the bad news. I was convinced the Brig wouldn't get round to it. I really didn't mean to put them through all that…" His voice trailed off. He took a sip of his beer, put his hands behind his head and leant back in his seat.

"It's OK. I know about that already. You weren't to know what dirty tricks they'd be up to Ellis." Carla sounded calm and reassuring. "You were just doing what you thought was right at the time. Obviously it'll be a real shock for them when they do find out I'm still around. Me and Lemmy have talked about it. He's going to break the news to them first, before I actually meet up with them. Anyway, we should be thanking you. You're the one who pieced together the story of what led to Rebecca's dreadful death and you're also the one who nailed our boss. We can't thank you enough for that. He was such a bastard!"

Ellis was surprised by the vehemence of Carla's reference to Daid and thought that there must be another part of the story that he was unaware of.

Toller returned with Carla's lager.

"Bloody queues! I'll leave you to it Ellis. No doubt you need time for a wee private discussion. I'll be over there keeping that robbing machine company." He walked across to a recess at the far end of the room where the one-armed bandits were flashing and beeping.

Carla was feeling uncomfortable. She'd only just met up with Ellis and now she had to get him to agree to attend a meeting with the Brigade. Before she could speak, Lemmy asked her what story she was going to tell her boss about how she'd managed to track down Ellis.

"I'm assuming you're not going to tell them that I led you to him!"

"Well, it did cross my mind to drop you in it like that," Carla replied, smiling. "But I thought the better way would be to tell them I'd contacted Lorna and persuaded her to tell me where Ellis was holed up – for his own good of course."

"I think they might buy that. By the way, what exactly happened with that explosion at your place? It sounded a little serious."

Ellis, who'd begun to drift off, was suddenly all ears.

"Oh that. I suppose you don't get all the gossip out in the field. It was a young lad apparently – a nutter obviously. God knows what he was after. But by the time the hierarchy had got on to the case, it had become a full scale terrorist attack."

Carla had dropped her voice, conscious that their conversation was drifting into a very sensitive area. She glanced around to check they weren't being overheard. But the boxing match on the sports channel was the only thing attracting attention in the bar.

"The lad was shot and killed for his pains – by the security guards. We weren't supposed to find out, but one of them blabbed. They reckoned there must have been others involved but the enquiry got nowhere. It didn't help that the cameras down in the tunnel weren't working."

Ellis already knew that Toller had tried to blow up the underground entrance to the Darkstone HQ, but it was a moment before he took in the last part of what Carla had said. The cameras weren't working! That meant Toller was in the clear.

"Sorry Ellis, you'll have to excuse all this shop talk. Lemmy and I haven't seen each other for a while and we're just catching up. But there's something I need to ask you, a big favour really."

Carla told him about the conversation she'd had with her boss. "I know I said up at your house that I'd keep the information about your film secret. Well, once you'd escaped, things were about to go ballistic. I figured I needed something to disarm them. So I told my boss about the film."

Ellis was about to flare up, but Lemmy calmed him and asked him to hear Carla out.

"I admit that telling him about the film was a risk. But I think it gives you a position of strength. I thought it was the best way of securing your freedom. Maybe I was wrong but that was my judgement."

Ellis didn't know what to make of all this. It was too much information, too quickly. She had made a promise about the film and had broken it. He'd been conned once and didn't want to risk it happening again. Could he trust her this time? Or maybe he could use it to his advantage. The other two waited for Ellis to respond. He took another sip of beer and cleared his throat.

"I can see why you told them. It was probably a good move. What needs to happen next?"

Carla breathed a sigh of relief. "Well my boss wants you to

come in for a meeting. You won't be under arrest and you'll be free to go afterwards. I think he wants to make a deal with you – after all you have some very dangerous ammunition. He's also promised to release your friend Ross and to drop the charges against him. What do you think? Are you willing to meet the boss?"

Ellis knew he had no real option. If he walked away now, he'd be in limbo, not knowing how things would turn out, being at risk of re-arrest. If he went along with their proposal, he'd be able to bargain and, as Carla had said, he was well armed.

"I'll do it. When do we meet?"

For the second time Carla looked relieved. "I'll need to phone my boss, but probably tomorrow afternoon. I think you've made the right decision. Just one thing though. Don't for God's sake mention that you met me and Lemmy together. Officially we don't know each other and have never had any contact."

"That won't be a problem," Ellis said. His pie had gone cold but that didn't stop him finishing it off.

"Good man, Ellis." Lemmy was clearly pleased about Ellis' decision. "Do you fancy a little walk? I've a couple of things in my bag I need to tell you about. They may be useful for your meeting – a few more bargaining chips."

"That sounds intriguing. But first, I need to phone Lorna and tell her what's happening and I need a quick word with Toller to see if it's OK to stay at his relative's place tonight."

"See you outside in five minutes then." Lemmy stood up and looked suddenly serious. "There's something I have to tell you both. After today, you won't be seeing me again. I'm going away."

Carla and Ellis were completely thrown, but Lemmy didn't explain.

+ + +

Lorna sat side by side with Laska on the sofa. Ellis didn't allow him on any of the seats at home, but she felt she could make up her own rules up in the flat.

The journey into Glasgow with Gam had been long and tedious. He'd spent the whole time telling her how difficult it would be for him to run a feature on Ellis and his revelations about Commander Daid. Lorna knew about Gam's history with the Brig and that he literally had the scars to prove it. But he didn't seem to have the courage of his own convictions. He was dedicated, inventive and resourceful, but when it came to the really big issues, Lorna felt he wanted to hide under the bed and wait for things to go away. When they'd reached the flats, he'd still been vacillating, unsure what to do. He'd said he'd let her know when he'd come to a conclusion.

She'd then had to spend the best part of an hour on the phone to the Brigade's Registration Section explaining why she hadn't responded to their messages. Where had she been? Why had she not informed them she was going away? Who had she been with? She wondered which of her neighbours had reported her absence. But she had her story ready and explained that she'd been at her mother's flat, that her mother had been ill and that there'd been no time to call the Brigade to update them on her movements. Of course they'd insisted on asking her mother to verify these details. Lorna had briefed her mother well and the Brigade had backed off.

She got up from the sofa to feed Laska and thought about Ellis. She'd been so lucky to have had that first chance encounter with him. She missed him dreadfully and hoped that Lemmy would be able to keep her man away from the clutches of the Brigade. Even from her one very brief meeting with Lemmy she felt confidence in him. She scooped biscuit and some small pieces of chicken into Laska's bowl and watched as he devoured the food.

As she hadn't heard anything from Gam, Lorna decided to take the initiative and went in search of some technical help. She walked up the two flights to Colette's flat and luckily found her in and Gam out. It was a relief that there was no need to confront him.

"Look, this is a bit awkward, Colette. I really want to write a piece about the woman who Ellis found and get it on the Net. I don't know if Gam has said anything to you but he's not keen to get involved. That's fine and I understand. But I still want to go ahead and need some help."

"OK." Colette said. "Could you fill me in on what's happened? Gam was pretty vague about it."

"I can do better than that. I can give you a film show, but I warn you it's very unsettling."

Lorna took the disc out of her pocket and slotted it into Colette's player. She gave a running commentary to explain what was happening, as Colette watched the flickering images open-mouthed. When the film ended, Lorna took out her phone and showed Colette the picture of the wolf and the Brigade Commander.

Colette was speechless. Her worst suspicions about the Brigade were confirmed.

Lorna was a little nervous. "I realise Gam doesn't want to run with the article and I thought perhaps we could do it together. I mean I don't know enough about the technical stuff, whereas you…"

Colette sighed and shrugged her shoulders. "Yes, he's become very cautious. I think the Brig have got to him. To be honest, I shouldn't get involved either. I've had warnings at work, you know, about what Gam's been up to. I could easily lose my job and Gam earns next to nothing. But, but, but! Having seen that film, I can't not do it. When do we start?"

"No time like the present. Shall we go down to mine?"

January 10th

Michael Cutting couldn't remember the last time he'd been in Edinburgh, or out of London for that matter. Normally he summoned everyone to the Pyramid. Cormack had briefed him by phone on the Commander's death. When Cormack called him again, to tell him about Landsman's explosive film, Cutting decided that his presence was required north of the border.

Just before he boarded the agency's private jet at the City of London airport, Cormack had texted him about a blog that had just surfaced on the 'Can of Worms' site, featuring an article about the life and death of Rebecca Leuchars. The late Commander had an all-too-starring role in the story.

Cutting briefly delayed his departure so that his PA could join him. They worked on the media release on the flight north. By the time they arrived at Edinburgh airport, where they were met by Cormack, his earlier anger had dissipated. He felt back in control.

His PA took a taxi to the SecureScotland HQ, to arrange the issue of the media release. But Cutting felt like some fresh air. Their car took them to the foot of Arthur's seat. The path up to the summit was a good place to talk without interruption or fear of eavesdropping. He and Cormack made their way slowly uphill, stopping frequently to catch their breath and admire the view.

"Before we get on to the difficult business, I want to congratulate you, Iain, on your success in using Landsman to skewer the late Commander. I appreciate his death was an unexpected development, but dangerous dogs can be so unpredictable. Your work puts us in a strong position to respond to the coverage of Leuchars."

Cutting glanced at the breaking news website on his phone. "I see the nationals are already snapping at our heels, so we need to move fast. My PA will release our response within the next hour. Our line is the classic case of the single bad apple. We'll tell them that as a result of the findings of your investigation, Iain, we had been about to arrest and charge the Commander."

"So we'll present the catalogue of evidence we've amassed, showing the Commander in the worst possible light?"

"Precisely, Iain. Had the dog not stepped in, so to speak, the man would have been under arrest and trial and conviction would have followed. We can show the full extent of our investigations and demonstrate that the rot goes no further than Daid. However I've decided that this situation gives us an excellent opportunity to carry out a little re-organisation, things we should perhaps have done some time ago. You remember we touched on this when you were last in London. We'll home in on SecureScotland's lack of control and oversight of the Commander. With Mr Pelham gone, there'll be nobody senior to contradict us. I intend to close down SecureScotland. The nationalists won't like it, but we'll just tell them they had their chance and blew it."

Cormack wasn't surprised. He'd expected this from Cutting and it made a lot of sense.

"We'll manage the commissioning and oversight from the Pyramid and I want you there in overall control, Iain."

This, he hadn't expected. But a return to London would give him scope to spread his wings. Before he had a chance to say anything, Cutting continued. He lowered his voice although there was nobody to be seen on the steep path upwards.

"I also want you to run Darkstone from the Pyramid. It needs a tighter rein. From the information you've provided, it's clear that Mr Pelham allowed Morrisey to give his agents carte blanche. I've no problem with the principle of our security professionals having very considerable leeway to do what they need to do, but it needs to be properly controlled. The way it's been operating leaves us unnecessarily vulnerable should there be any leaks."

Cormack looked out towards the Firth of Forth. The sun was pleasantly warm and he undid his fleece. It was good to know that he and Cutting thought along very similar lines.

"I have to say I'm really pleased with your proposals, sir. I've missed being at the Pyramid and Glasgow can be a little provincial at times."

Together they struggled up to the stony peak and took a few minutes to recover.

"You have to hand it to Landsman," Cutting said. "He may be a complete amateur but he's played an excellent game. He's in a strong position. It's a great pity we didn't know about the film before you brought him in. But we are where we are."

Cormack took this comment as the criticism it was intended to be. He'd underestimated Landsman.

Cutting continued. "I agree that we should work out a deal with the man. We don't want him running around as a potential future threat, ready to pull the pin on his evidence grenade at anytime. What's the news on his whereabouts?"

"I've just heard that he's been traced. Good work by our agent. In fact he's here in the city so I've arranged to use one of the interview rooms at SecureScotland for our little discussion. I assume you'll want to observe." Cutting nodded. "I've arranged for the car to pick us up at Duddingston, just down there." Cormack pointed to the cluster of buildings in the distance. "So we can be back in town in good time."

As they walked down the far side of the hill, Cutting thought about the changes he'd be introducing. The number one decision was to manage Darkstone from London. He knew he should really have done this from the start. But Pelham had been so damn persuasive at the time about local management – really as a sop to the nationalists. Cormack would put a halt to the more extreme actions. But, people had very short memories and terrorist outrages would continue to happen. After a decent interval, he'd give Cormack the green light to reintroduce Darkstone's extra-curricular activity – under proper controls of course.

Cutting's second step would be to merge the Strathclyde and Forth contracts. He knew this is what Daid had been planning and with the Commander out of the picture this would leave Chen as top dog. His tough, no nonsense approach was just what was needed. He was not a man to be easily distracted. Daid of course had been quite the opposite.

And number three on the list would be the closure of SecureScotland. He mentally totted up the combined savings that his plans would generate and rubbed his hands. Less cost and more control. It was just how he liked it – devolving power was just a costly distraction.

"One thing I meant to mention, Iain. I was impressed how you managed to get the formula just right."

"Which formula would that be?"

"You know, the stuff that Daid used. He must have thought he'd succeeded in taking Landsman out of the picture. But you managed to get the balance just right."

"Well, I had some practice in the old days. Some skills you never lose."

They reached the lower slopes of the hill and walked slowly to the village. As they passed the pub they were both tempted to divert, but neither of them said a word. The car was waiting and they slid into the comfortable rear seats for their journey to the SecureScotland office.

+ + +

Cutting glanced at the headline of the Globe Online article – 'The Cocaine Commander and the Call Girl'. He lifted his eyes from the screen and looked through the glass to the room beyond. He watched unseen as Major Cormack and Ellis Landsman took their seats.

"My guess is that it was you who sent me those texts, but I don't suppose you'll want to comment on that. You must have had your own reasons for nailing Daid." Ellis didn't feel any need to hold back. From what Carla and Lemmy had told him, he was in a strong position.

"You're right. I couldn't possibly comment. But let's get on with the matter in hand. We know about your film. What we don't know is what you intend to do with it. Of course it's much less of a problem to us now. As you've surmised, we were pursuing the late Commander in any event. We'd like to find a way forward that is to our mutual benefit. What we want from you is your agreement not to use the film, in any way. What would you like in return?"

"I'd like you to close down Darkstone."

Cormack was completely thrown by Landsman's bald statement. Behind the glass Cutting thought momentarily about joining Cormack but decided against it. He was confident his man could handle the situation.

"And what would Darkstone be?"

"An undercover operation using dirty tricks, assassinations and disappearances, to enforce a zero tolerance security agenda.

It operates from a base under Central Station." Ellis was pleased with this particular piece of detection work.

"And what evidence do you have for such a bizarre claim?"

Ellis reached into his pocket and placed a small digital recorder on the table.

"This is part of my evidence. Do you want me to play it now or would you prefer that your colleague behind the glass didn't hear it?" This was an inspired guess on Ellis' part and he could tell from Cormack's involuntary glance towards the two-way mirror that he'd guessed right.

Cormack recovered his composure. "Go ahead and play it."

Ellis switched the machine on and Cormack heard his own voice echoing across the room.

I've carried out a little research of my own. In all cases where there's been a fatality, there's been a clear self defence justification.

Ellis stopped the tape and wound forward slightly.

If you were to raise these concerns again in any forum, you would be subject to immediate dismissal.

Cormack remembered the conversation only too well. But he'd not gone out on a limb. He felt justified in everything he'd said that day. "How did you obtain this confidential information Mr Landsman?"

"From a very helpful man called Lemmy, one of your agents, I understand. But what is a little more worrying from your point of view, is that he also provided me with a copy of a detailed report on the deaths you mentioned on the tape. Not one of those deaths can be justified as self-defence. Darkstone is clearly out of control and that's why it needs to be closed down. I can let you have a copy of that report by the way." Ellis leaned back in his chair. "Would there be any chance of a glass of water?"

Cormack left the room and met up with Cutting in the adjoining office.

"He gets more impressive as time goes on doesn't he, Iain?"

Cormack was surprised by Cutting's calmness. "How the fuck has he got hold of all this and what's happened to Charlesworth? I knew his CV looked suspicious. What sort of game has he been playing?"

"So Lemmy is his nickname is it? How quaint" Cutting said. "Look it's a worry but don't forget this all happened under the old watch. It was all supposed to be under Pelham's control. He's dead, we're closing SecureScotland, you were investigating Darkstone and from what Landsman's said, we've found some highly incriminating evidence. Result! It's no real problem if we close Darkstone down in Scotland. We can resurrect it to operate in London. We know what to avoid. You'll be in control after all. And he won't know a thing about what we do down there."

Cormack could see that this made a lot of sense.

"Go back in and tell him we need to see that report and verify what he's told us. If it checks out we'll agree to his request. In the meantime you need to find out where Charlesworth is."

+ + +

Ellis sat and reflected on a successful outcome. His plan had worked well – thanks mainly to Lemmy's evidence. He phoned Lorna to tell her he was a free man and that he'd be staying the night in Edinburgh, with yet another of Toller's relatives. He said he was exhausted, but would be OK after a good night's rest.

As Toller drove him to his cousin's place in Craigmillar, Ellis told him the good news about the cameras in the tunnel, or rather, their absence.

Lorna, Colette and Laska went out to Kintrawe, in the darkness, in the ailing Transit, to warm the house up.

January 11th

Toller dropped Ellis off near Kintrawe and disappeared to Alexandria to see a woman. Ellis walked up the track towards home, breathing in the fresh winter air, trying to remove the city fumes from his lungs. He arrived at the house and spotted Lorna and Colette stacking logs in the woodshed. He shouted out to the two women.

"You two did a great job. That article on Rebecca was brilliant!"

"Ellis!" Lorna shouted, ran to him, threw her arms around his neck and kissed him. "We didn't hear a car arriving. How did you get here?"

"Oh, I just walked the last mile or so – needed the fresh air. Toller has gone back to Alexandria to meet a woman. He likes to push it, but good luck to him."

"How did you know it was us two who'd written the article?" Colette asked him.

"Lemmy told me you'd spoken to him. By the way he's gone."

"What do you mean gone?"

"He's left the country, don't ask me where he's going, he wouldn't tell me. All I know is he kind of burnt his boats with the Brigade so it was time for him to disappear. But not before giving me some ammunition which I've just used very successfully I think." He explained to them about the deal he'd reached.

"So they'll close Darkstone down?"

"That's what they said. After all, as I told them, if I get a sniff of anything going on I'll release Lemmy's evidence to the media. By the way, how's Gam taken it – I mean about you two usurping his role?"

Colette smiled. "Oh, he's still sulking of course but he'll get over it. He knows he can't afford to live without my money."

* January 11th

They've actually released Ross Lambert. Great news! Can't really say I expected it to happen.

I'm still recovering from two shocks. The first was about Aran. At the end of Lambert's hearing, as he was leaving the room to be taken into custody, he brushed past me and slipped a piece of paper into my suit pocket. I don't think anybody else noticed. He didn't say a word. In all the excitement that followed, I forgot all about it. I didn't wear that suit jacket again until yesterday. I was looking for a tissue in the pocket and pulled out the note. It contained one brief phrase – 'Cormack is Aran's brother'. I've no idea how he found out. I never suspected a thing. Aran's never given any indication that she has a relative in the Brigade. Far from it – she's always been a bit sniffy about the organisation. I should have realised there was something odd when Cormack said he'd informed Aran himself about my 'death'. No wonder! I'm afraid I flew at Aran when we managed to meet up. I told her you don't keep that sort of secret from your lover to which she replied it had been for my own good. That only made things worse. I stormed out.

Shock number two was Lemmy. He showed me the Darkstone dossier he'd been working on. He's checked out the four deaths we knew about and not one of them could be justified as self-defence. He told me he'd given a copy of the report to Ellis for him to confront C with. But then he played me the audio tape. The man only went and wired himself for his meeting with Cormack in Ferguson House!

On the tape, C sounded very dismissive about Lemmy's evidence. Doesn't put him in a good position if any of this leaks out publicly. Lemmy gave me a copy of his dossier and the tape. I've given it to Val my legal guy who's passed it on to a third party for safe keeping. He won't tell me who, quite rightly.

I saw the blog article about Rebecca Leuchars. Whoever wrote it is a hero. Good to hear someone else had the same view of Daid that I did. But of course I didn't suffer like poor Rebecca. I feel a strange kind of bond with her.

Anyway – back to Lemmy. He saved the best till last. After the meet up with Ellis we left the pub and walked up to Morningside and across the Meadows. It's really nice there. He was telling me he'd been undercover for fifteen years. When I asked him how long he'd been in the Brigade for, he told me fifteen years. I couldn't work this out, as he couldn't have started off undercover. It's a minimum of five years before you're allowed that role. I asked him what he meant. He told me he was undercover when he joined the Brig. There were three of them, called themselves the Underground, made a really long term decision, all about undermining the Brig from the inside. He said he'd never told anybody else. What trust! I could be tempted with Lemmy, but somehow I don't think it would work. I need to get back in touch with Aran. Maybe her secret wasn't that important.

But teaming up with Lemmy won't be possible, even if I wanted to. He's gone – left the country, told me it was time for a change. Fifteen years was long enough. I hope he finds sanctuary somewhere.

I'm meeting up with mother and father tomorrow. Lemmy saw them and broke the news, just before he disappeared. We'll be in a small hotel. I couldn't bear to go home.

February 1st

They were felling in the wood at the far end of Ellis' land. The snow had returned. Toller was leading the horse down a slope between two stands of trees when he saw the body.

"Boss!" he shouted, trying to make himself heard over the wind. There was no reply. He tethered the horse and walked back to the crest of the hill where they'd had their sandwiches. Ellis was still there, stacking some shorter lengths of timber.

"You'd better come." The two of them walked heads down to avoid the swirls of snow. Toller offered Ellis a cigarette and they blew smoke up into the grey sky.

There, lying in the snow at the foot of an enormous spruce, was Lucas, a thin shadow of his former self. They instinctively took their hats off and stood with heads bowed.

"He must have finally run out of food – a sad way to go. Come on, let's get some tools and give him a decent burial. We don't want him being dug up for someone else to eat now do we?"

They walked back to the house and grabbed a couple of spades, a pickaxe and some thick plastic sheeting. The ground was hard and unyielding, progress slow. They sweated away, stopping briefly for another smoke. Eventually Ellis was satisfied with the depth. He carefully wrapped the wolf in the sheeting and placed him in the grave. He said a few words, thanking the wolf for his company. Toller added the experience to his already long list of Ellis eccentricities and filled in the grave. Ellis stood silently at first and then his lips began to move. He thanked Lucas for dealing with Daid so effectively and then turned to face a figure to his left.

"I was wondering where you'd been. Thought perhaps you'd buggered off, found better things to do."

"*No, no. I've just been taking a bit of a rest. Takes it out of me you know all this chat! So the boy's coming on well I see.*"

"Sure is. I don't know what I'd have done without him. Can't see him staying much longer, but you never know."

"*And what about the lassie? Will she be sticking around?*"

"God, I hope so. I don't fancy going back to Mr Lonesome. What about yourself?"

But when Ellis looked up to catch his father's reply, he'd gone.

Acknowledgements

Thanks to Gabrielle, Polly, Rob, Emma and the Writers' Lunch Group.

SHORELINE

Harry Vos and a woman walking her dog are shocked
to discover the body of a young man on an otherwise
deserted Belgian beach.

When Harry returns to the beach, after phoning the police,
he's completely thrown to discover that
the BODY,
the WOMAN
and her DOG
have all disappeared...